The Shipyard Murders

BY ADELE LANGENDORF

The Shipyard Murders

BY ADELE LANGENDORF

Though I researched many books on WWII Home Front America before writing this book, it is a work of fiction. The story comes first, though I tried to honor historical facts while creating purely fictional characters.

To Don, my love, my fan and cheerleader.
Together we achieve our dreams.

Who can fill the gap? You!
You women can give our boys what they need!

—*March of Time Newsreel, 1941*

Chapter One

Helen wrapped her fingers around five-year-old Amy's hand, panicked that they would get separated among the masses of shipyard workers coming out of the rows of identical apartments. There were many jokes about the bland complex, the most frequent one being: "If you came home drunk one night, you could walk into your neighbor's apartment." From the noises she had heard in the building, Helen would not have wanted to wander into her neighbors' apartments. Helen's limit was an occasional Whiskey Sour, and she hadn't had even one of those since moving to Vanport. She was alone with Amy, and had come here to do a job.

Amy tugged at Helen's arm. But Helen didn't mind. Amy's eagerness to go to her new preschool made her seem happy, already well-adjusted, alleviating Helen's guilt over her divorce and over having taken Amy away from California. Though Amy had known all the children at the private preschool back in California, and the classes there were smaller, she preferred the more creative Kaiser school where they drew unlimited amounts of pictures, sang the alphabet song, and the playground was large with slides, ladders, and tricycles to ride.

Helen walked with Amy to the child-care kindergarten's red brick building and watched her join the other children. Their laughter remained in her mind as she boarded one of the many buses exclusively for workers. Oregon shipbuilding was three miles from Vanport, though the distance seemed longer than that the few times Helen had walked there. Masses of men and women pushed and shoved each other as they stepped off the bus and trudged toward their stations in the yard. The stale tobacco smell melded with the licorice aroma of melted tar. A general sound of mixed voices sounded like static on a radio.

The bus from downtown had arrived at the same time, and Helen's friend, Charlotte, stepped off while Helen waited for her. They had met at a brief welding class for workers at Benson High School and since then often got together for dinner or coffee. Charlotte's friend Roxanne called, "Wait for me," as she hurried to catch up with them.

Helen tried not to stare at Roxanne's smudged mascara that looked like dirt on her face, but couldn't help comparing her to Charlotte with her skin smooth as porcelain and a touch of blue shadow on each eyelid.

Charlotte pulled herself up to her maximum height, as though she were trying to intimidate Roxanne. "Were you with Erich again last night?"

"Just stop it," Roxanne said. "Leave me alone." She sounded like a spoiled child.

Charlotte insisted, "I worry about you. He's not a nice person. Besides, he's married."

Roxanne pouted. "He's going to tell her tonight that he wants a divorce."

Charlotte laughed. "How many times has he promised this?"

"Golly, Charlotte, I know you don't like him but he makes me feel loved," Roxanne said as she moved toward the administration building where she was a secretary. Helen felt as though she were eavesdropping on a family conversation, something private that she shouldn't have overheard. "See you later," she said, trying to treat this like a normal get-together.

Helen joined the other workers heading for their stations in assembly buildings and on partially built ships. The heat of the crowd penetrated her body. People bumped into her; some even stepped on her feet. They fascinated Helen. She had never known any Negroes, or ever seen such deeply tobacco-stained fingers, or met young girls working to earn their college tuition. This was one of the reasons she had come here: to leave her sheltered little world behind and find out firsthand what else there was to the world.

The panorama of administration, assembly, storage, and plating buildings, of long concrete paths, covered bus stops, cars, and buses floated like a hurricane. Delivery scooters and gigantic cranes whizzed by, dangerously close. The other workers folded into shadows. Confronted by the chaos, Helen felt her optimism fade into something darker as she recalled the other reason why she'd fled California, taking her child out of a 2500-square-foot home on a quiet street in Atherton, California, and bringing her to a tiny apartment in this wild, crazy environment: because she had found her husband in bed with another woman, because she had learned that he sold tires on the black market, and because she wanted a new life, one in which Amy was not exposed to her father's dishonorable values. For all those reasons, she was willing to be scorned by her acquaintances for instigating a divorce.

One step in front of the other, Helen told herself. She thought of the union card in her wallet and of an advertisement from the newspaper for immediate employment at the Oregon shipyard. Two weeks before the end of the required time in Reno for her divorce, she had made the phone call and her future was sealed, a new life, hopefully one she would not regret.

She was part of the scene, one of the workers helping win the war against Japan. Of all the yards, Oregon Shipbuilding Corporation built the most ships in the shortest time. It was something to be proud of. Of course she would not regret her decision.

Helen stopped at her locker to pick up her welding helmet, protective suede jacket, and gloves, then continued on to the almost-completed Liberty ship where she worked. It was the first in the row of the five that had moved from the slipways to the berths in the Willamette River for the final welding, painting, and electrical work.

Painters and cleaners had climbed up the rigging to work on the outside of the ship while welders and electricians, who worked in various other locations on the ship, used the rigging as a faster means of boarding. Not Helen. The steps were bad enough: narrow without a banister or any kind of rod to hold onto.

Taking deep breaths, as she had every morning, Helen hoped to gain the courage to climb up to her station. An odor of dampness and mold assaulted her. A whirly crane lifted a side of the three-deck-house, swung it through the air, and delivered it to the main deck.

That's all she needed. Her breath came in short spurts. Inhale and exhale, she reminded herself, repeating her breathing exercise. Finally, she grabbed a bar of the rigging with her left hand and placed her right foot on the first step. Next, she reversed to right hand and left foot. She continued stepping in this cautious and steady manner until she reached halfway to the ship's deck and made the mistake of looking down.

Helen squeezed the rigging with both hands and forced herself to look up again. Just as she did, something hurtled through the air and spiraled downward. It was a person. She watched its trajectory as it kept going like a pilot without a parachute and splashed into the water, disappearing into the Willamette River.

Men and women scrambled to climb down the rigging, leaving the deck empty, while Helen stood frozen halfway to the top. Only one person remained. It was either a small man or a woman in workclothes and it sprinted across the deck. Probably a woman, Helen concluded, because she walked like a ballerina, the way Charlotte did.

The sight flustered Helen into feeling she should be on firm ground. She hastened down the steps to the planking and joined the bystanders, who had congregated at the river's edge. Some lit their cigarettes while others, who had been walking by, stopped at the edge of the river to peer into its cold depths.

A small boat moved in circles around the water. One of the guardsmen, wearing a wetsuit, dove from the boat and disappeared underwater, sending ripples to the surface. There followed the sound of agitated voices, everyone speaking at once.

"Who was it?" someone said. Another onlooker asked, "What happened?"

Helen moved as close as she could get to the river where the other workers were shoving each other. She was happy to be small, able to maneuver through the crowd and go largely unnoticed. She moved forward between some men and women and around others until she was only a few feet from the river's edge, where she dug her feet into the ground and refused to budge. Someone offered her a cigarette, which she lit and inhaled, hoping the tobacco would calm her. It choked her instead.

Sirens sounded. Red and white lights infused the area like reflections on the screen at a drive-in movie. An ambulance and a sheriff's car pulled up. The ambulance driver and his assistant rolled a stretcher to the water's edge, where they and the sheriff waited for the Coast Guardsmen to deliver the victim.

The boat pulled up to the shoreline and one Guardsman climbed ashore and held the boat while his partner lifted what appeared to be a man, limp as a string puppet, from the boat. His water-soaked coveralls clung to him. They placed him on the stretcher where one technician breathed into the man's mouth while the other massaged his heart. After breathing and massaging for a frantic five minutes, they gave up.

"He's a goner. Call the coroner."

"Not so fast," the sheriff said as he examined the face. "Looks like he hit his head or someone hit him before he fell."

The ambulance technician scrutinized the dead man's forehead. "The wound here must a' been from a small tool, like a wrench or pliers. Someone hit him, all right. Got the victim's name?"

"Some guy identified him as Erich Cranston," the sheriff answered. "The coroner will verify that."

A few workers in front of Helen spoke in unison. "That's Erich. He's a lead electrician."

Other bystanders all said the same thing, their voices sounding like an echo. "Who will replace him? Not any of these girls."

A man approached the group and said, "I'm the most experienced. I deserve to be foreman."

Another man towered over the first one. "Who made you God? I was doing electrical work before you were born."

"Well, Grandpa, did your stupid brain think you might be too old for the job?"

A heaviness in the air promised rain. Or was it the barely mourned death of the worker that caused Helen to feel the weight?

"Shut up," she said. It felt good to swear, though she knew such language was unbecoming. It relieved her tension. "Don't you have any respect for the dead?"

"We're being practical," the younger man said. "We got a schedule to keep."

The sight of the attendants rolling the stretcher within inches of the two men relieved Helen's tension. For a moment she imagined they would bump into the thoughtless men.

The coroner parked his truck and moved to the stretcher, where he began his examination. The absence of a siren imitated the silence of death. Workers climbed back up the rigging and steps. Ships and workers floated around Helen. The spinning froze her to the ground. She knew that she should get back to her station. The factory worked in assembly lines; everyone had to do their part for operations to run smoothly. But that knowledge didn't help her move.

She looked at the sky to compose herself. Was there a Heaven? Her brother could be looking down at her with disapproval, not wanting to see his sister as a shipyard worker. When he and his friends had played football in the street, Helen had watched the pigskin soar through the air, longing to get out there with them and throw or catch the ball. He told her this was not a game for girls and when she tried on his baseball mitt, he had grabbed it from her. It wasn't feminine.

He had been killed in the Battle of the Bulge, which took place in Belgium. Newsreels at the Paramount Theatre that depicted the battle had made Helen ill. The United States Army was trapped. German soldiers, who had hidden on every side of the entrance to the country, attacked the Americans. Thousands fell in bloody heaps. Helen had always wondered if her brother had lain there in searing pain while he bled to death or whether he had died instantly.

She was happy to work in a defense factory to honor his life, as well as to rise above the limitations forced on girls. She climbed up to her station on the main deck where she would weld steel sheets to strengthen the ship's bow.

When she first took the electrode holder in her hand, it shook. The memory of the dead body floated in her mind. This was dangerous work. Anyone on this ship could be injured or die. These thoughts could halt her work, but she wasn't going to let them. She was a competent arc welder. Blue sparks flew as she moved the rod along the steel pieces, using like metal to bond the seam. When she was finished, Helen wiped off the slush, stepped back and admired her work. Each time she completed a job, Helen marveled that she was able to accomplish such a feat towards sending a cargo ship to serve the troops overseas. A few months ago, she would never have been capable of these things, or believed in this vision of herself now: a welder, a woman working on behalf of her country.

Naval officers, sheriffs and other officials walked onto the deck, roped off the area where Erich had been murdered and huddled together to speak secretly.

One of the Coast Guard officers and a man wearing a dark suit with a badge on the lapel met briefly with the sheriff, who broke from them and spoke through a megaphone.

"This is a crime scene. Please stay at your stations and one of us will question you. Please cooperate."

Helen took deep breaths. She figured the man in a dark suit had to be FBI. She couldn't take her eyes off of him. No doubt the FBI had gotten involved because this was government property, but in her mind his presence verified that they were looking for a killer. Someone had hit Erich and thrown him overboard. The lack of the thrum of electrical connections, of noise from hammered metal, and the absence of blue sparks from welded steel seemed funereal. Helen couldn't move. Finally she managed to unplug her electrode holder.

Sheriffs, deputies, Naval personnel and Coast Guard officers maneuvered around, asking questions. Their silver badges brightened the dull gray ship. What would she say when they questioned her? It was her duty to answer honestly but she wasn't at all certain that the woman she had seen was Charlotte, or even that it was a woman.

Most of the deputies divided to question workers on the deck while others went below to question welders and electricians who worked in the officers' quarters. The deputies would have to call for the painters and cleaners to climb out of the ship's bottom and from the storage holds. Helen remembered that the women painters' helpers, who worked in the bottom of the boat, complained that they had to climb through a small hole and crawl on their hands and knees in the tiny area, dragging a light bulb on an extension chord, to scrape rust. They would have to crawl out and back inside again. She was happy not to do this work, exempt because she was well-educated and white.

A man wearing a star-shaped badge approached Helen. He introduced himself as Sheriff Graham. He appeared to be Helen's age, was stocky and needed a shave. Helen's eyes focused on the gun in a holster that was attached to his belt. Another sign of impending danger.

"Pardon me, Ma'am, I need to ask if you saw any unusual action on the ship around the time the dead man fell."

Helen closed her eyes and recalled the times she had walked with Charlotte to work and to and from many lunches. She opened her eyes and shook her head.

"Are you sure?"

"Well, I saw someone on the ship after everyone else was down below, but it was quite a distance and I couldn't see clearly."

"Sometimes if you try and review the scene in your mind you might remember more."

What should I do? Helen asked herself. Withholding evidence was as bad as lying to the police. Helen managed to say, "She walked like someone I work with, but again I'm really not sure I could say."

If it were Charlotte she had seen, would she find out that Helen had reported her? Helen looked around to check if anyone could hear her. The workers were either talking to deputies or waiting expectantly, their eyes on the other people being questioned.

"You seem to be hesitant," the sheriff said. "Let me assure you that we consider many reports and evidence before determining someone guilty."

Guilty? Innocent? Helen had to tell the truth. "It might have been Charlotte Yamamoto. She has a unique walk, like a ballerina."

He laughed, sounding like a fake Santa Claus. "Honey, we don't have any ballerinas in the shipyard."

Helen was relieved that he didn't take her seriously until she saw him write something in his notebook.

"We'll check this out," he said, smirking as though he were already bored with her and what she had to say.

But he had written the name down and that worried Helen. "Maybe I was wrong. It might not have been anyone I know."

"We'll check out all of our evidence before coming to any conclusions."

Me and my big mouth, Helen thought. She wanted to pick each letter, like rotten fruit, and throw Charlotte's name away.

She watched the sheriff move on to someone else. The distance between her and the figure she had seen made it difficult to be certain. What if the sheriff told Charlotte that Helen had reported her? She abhorred women who spoke ill of their friends. She should have kept her mouth shut.

Chapter Two

Helen was running late because of the questioning. This was the worst night to go to her parents' house for dinner, but she could not cancel at the last minute. Her mother had asked them for dinner several times before Helen had finally accepted. After the way her mother had reacted when Helen told her she had left Edgar, she dreaded the evening. Her mother had thought that Edgar was a "good catch," coming from a nice Jewish family and having a bright future. Before they got married, he had already owned his own business.

She drove across the St. Johns Bridge and down 32nd Street, past her alma mater, Grant High School, a large brick building, surrounded by trees. It seemed like a century since she had walked down the hall, flirting with the boys, sitting through lectures and sweating over exams until she graduated.

"Do you think Grandpa will play like a horse with me?" Amy asked.

"You like that?" Helen asked, trying not to ignore Amy but distracted by the familiar territory, which made her nostalgic.

"He's funny and I like Grandma's cookies."

They passed the corner where she and her friends had played kick the can in the street, and Mrs. Fulton's house where they used to ice skate on her frozen fishpond. The lady was on her parents' party line and the girls would go to Helen's house and listen to Mrs. Fulton and her friends talking on the phone.

This was during the Depression, and doubling up was one way the phone company could reduce customer rates. Her mother complained and her dad used his influence, as a senator, to obtain a single line. Now, with war work causing an influx of factory workers, they were forced to share a party line again. To complain would be unpatriotic. Helen derived wicked pleasure from this. She cringed every time her mother thought they were entitled to privileges denied to the "common folks."

Lights shone out from the brick house on the corner, from the stucco residence across the street, and from both porches and every room in the white colonial house where she had grown up, lighting the green shutters. Her parents had blackout shades, which, since they didn't live on the coast, were hidden under cornices to be pulled down in case of an emergency.

"Mommy, do you like Grandma's cookies?" Amy said in an imperative voice.

"Yummy," she said, chagrined that her memories had interfered with their conversation. "We're here. Maybe Grandma baked some cookies for you."

The row of rosebushes bloomed yellow, pink and fuchsia, some in buds and others in full bloom, with petals lavish as a velvet gown. The robust foliage of Daphne bushes that stood on either side of the porch made Helen long to be the child who had turned somersaults on the sloping lawn.

Her father opened the door and kissed Helen's cheek. He seemed to get shorter every time she saw him. Brill Cream in his hair sparkled under the porch light. He lifted Amy up and placed her on his shoulders. Amy's laughter filled the room as they made a circle from the hall to the living room and back. He swished her through the air and placed her, feet first, on the floor. Amy rushed over to hug Sam, the Cocker Spaniel, who put his paws on her arms and licked her face.

"I want a dog. When can I have a dog, Mommy?" Amy asked, still hugging the dog.

"When we get a larger place, we'll have a puppy, I promise."

"We could have brought Tammy with us. Her ears are just like the puppies I like," Amy said.

She observed Amy, so vulnerable in her pale green dress with the smocked embroidery on her chest and her black patent leather Mary Jane shoes. Her large eyes locked with Helen's in a gesture of faith.

At that moment Helen was overwhelmed with the thought that she had such power to make her daughter happy or sad. Had she thought enough of Amy's well-being when she had planned to come to Oregon? Was her reasoning about taking Amy away from her father's corrupt values just a pep talk to reassure herself that leaving was necessary? Helen hugged Amy, inhaling the Johnson's Baby Shampoo scent in her hair.

She had thought about moving from Vanport. It had not been the delightful place she had pictured. Only a few of the roads were paved. The rest were gravel and spread dust like smoke rising from a burnt dinner. Drunken brawls and cranky residents were not providing the camaraderie that she had originally imagined. But Amy would have to wait for a dog and Helen would have to put up with the conditions. The influx of defense workers to Portland had made it impossible to rent any lodging.

Helen followed her father back to the living room where he sat on one of the two teal blue upholstered chairs, his feet planted on the Oriental rug, and leaned his body toward the Philco radio. He ingested every word coming through the chorded cloth of the curved mahogany case.

After heavy losses, German U-Boats in the Pacific disappeared."

"Serves those animals right," her father said, waving his forefinger at the radio.

Helen looked at the blond hair on the back of his hands. When she used to watch him wash his hands, it looked like his skin was peeling off. On his head, the hair had turned fluffy white and a few more wrinkles had sprouted around his eyes. He still wore his pants belted above his waist. She remembered when she and her brother used to make fun of the belt's position.

While he listened to the radio, he took a handkerchief from his pocket and blew his nose. It sounded like ocean waves.

He turned toward Helen. "Little one, I hope you and Amy will move back here."

"Dad, I'm 30 and you still call me Little One."

He laughed. "You'll always be our little one."

Helen never could resist his deep throaty laugh, although his remark still made her feel smothered.

Her mother called to Helen from the kitchen, none too soon. If she had stayed with him much longer, she might have shown her irritation and then who knew what words would've come out. "Little One" itself wasn't so bad. But to Helen the term of endearment described the way her parents treated her. Her mother had picked her up at grammar school every day while she walked the long way around the schoolyard so none of her friends would see her. And Helen had never left the house without her father telling her to be careful.

The minute Helen entered the kitchen, she felt the blast of heat from the oven as her mother took out the roast beef, placed it on a platter, and carried the pan over to the sink. She was wearing a striped housedress over her corseted body. Her gray hair contrasted with her flushed face. Her diamond ring cut into her flesh as she wrapped the fingers of one hand around a coffee can and held the roasting pan with the other. Helen watched the beef drippings flow into previously collected mushy fat and dribble into little tributaries. The soggy pile made Helen gag, though she knew the fat would be used to make ammunition for the armed forces.

"You're late," her mother said.

"Amy was poky." Helen had never lied to her mother before. She had withheld facts but never out and out lied. She swallowed a lump in her throat—because of the murder, because of her mother's red face and, most of all, because Helen hated to be dishonest with her. She hated keeping the news about the crime secret, but her parents already nagged her enough about working in the shipyard. She took the silver flatware and headed for the breakfast room.

"We're eating in the dining room tonight," her mother said as though sharing a secret.

"Is this a special occasion?"

"You'll see."

Holding the silver, Helen reversed her direction to the dining room and set the eating utensils on the linen-clad table. There were five plates, so Helen got another place setting, which she put by the extra plate.

"Mother, what's going on? It's not Passover and Elijah is not going to appear."

The doorbell rang.

"Would you get that, Honey?"

Helen opened the door to see Edgar, her ex-husband, standing on the porch. Every strand of his dark hair had been precisely cut. He wore a starched white shirt, Italian silk tie, and a dark suit. She wanted to blast her hand through the screen door and shove him down the stairs. Her face burned red-hot. Words like *leave this minute,* like *how dare you,* stuck in her throat. She slammed the door shut, took a deep breath, and opened it again.

Edgar walked inside. Her mother rushed to join them, her face flushed.

"Sorry I'm late, Mother Brooks."

"She's not your mother," Helen said.

"Helen," her mother said as though she were scolding a child. "Edgar, why don't you join Lloyd in the living room while we put food on the table. He is listening to the six o'clock news."

Listening to her mother fawn over Edgar caused Helen to feel as though she would burst. Remembering the first time she had met Edgar helped her understand how he had charmed her mother.

She and Edgar had almost bumped into each other at the Stanford Cellar, where Helen had gone for coffee between classes. At first glance, she noticed the little dots in his eyes that sparkled when he smiled. She was flattered when he called her the next day and they went to see *Charlie Chan at the Opera* at the Stanford Theatre and to Marquard's Drive-In for milkshakes.

After that first date, her friends had gathered around her, asking questions about him. He was a BMOC: Big Man on Campus. With his football player's build, polite manner and fun-loving personality, he had impressed all the women. Helen wasn't the only one he had fooled.

He had called her every day. When she returned to her room from class, she often saw the bobby pin dangling by a thread from the wall-buzzer, which meant she had missed a phone call. The vibration from the buzzer caused the pin to fall. The thrill that these calls might have come from Edgar had electrified Helen.

She remembered when other students had announced their engage-ments in the traditional way during dinner, with the Hasher placing a bouquet of roses, which reflected red hues on the crystal vase in front of them, happiness spilling tears from their wide eyes down their peach-colored cheeks to their smiling lips. Helen was thrilled when Edgar had proposed and she had received the same bouquet.

After that, she'd taken a class called Management in Relation to Family Living for engaged women and seniors, a class that covered compiling and budgeting a week's menu, recognizing fine china and linens, and identifying the cuts of meat from the figure of a cow, all of which she hated from the start.

Her first failure in preparation for her role as a homemaker had been the tray of popovers that came out burnt and inedible. She should have known then that she was no homemaker. But she didn't want to be an old maid. She'd been too young and too sheltered to conceive of other alternatives to these two fates.

After seven years of marriage she realized that Edgar was not such a great guy after all. She had walked in on her husband in their bedroom wrapping a sheet around his naked body, while his secretary grasped her clothes and black market nylon stockings to hide her indiscretion. Helen had ignored all the other loose women in his life until that moment.

Amy ran up to Edgar, crying, "Daddy, Daddy." She fell into his arms. He swung her up and kissed her forehead. A smile spread across her face. She giggled. Helen hadn't seen Amy sparkle like that for a long time. She wanted Amy to hate her father, a thought that immediately shamed her.

"Are you going to come home with us?" Amy asked.

"Not this time, Pumpkin," Edgar replied in a tragic voice.

"Please stay," Amy pleaded.

Helen tried to think about Amy's friends at school, about how eager she was to go to class each morning, but she couldn't blot the guilt out of her mind about taking Amy away from her father. Helen pictured Amy being pulled in two directions, with one arm yanked by Edgar and one by her. She struggled to come up with a solution that wouldn't hurt their daughter. "You can go stay with Daddy when school is out," Helen said.

Amy opened her eyes wide. "Will you come, too?"

Helen flushed. She had been cruel to her own daughter just to get even with Edgar. "We'll work it out."

In the kitchen, Helen's hand shook as she took the platter from her mother. "How could you invite him?"

"My hope was that by bringing you two back together, you'd leave this silliness behind and become a family again," her mother said, the tone of her voice an octave higher than usual. "Really, Helen. It's best for you and Amy to make amends."

Of course, Edgar was directed to sit next to Helen, but first he rushed to the head of the table and pulled out her mother's chair. She smiled at him. "Thank you, Darling."

Helen willed herself to be calm. Edgar sat down. On his other side, Amy sat on two cushions in her chair.

Helen's father carved the roast that she had placed in front of him, while everyone helped themselves to string beans and roasted potatoes from silver serving dishes. The roast must have cost her mother a month's worth of red ration stamps, just to impress Edgar or to show him her continued adoration.

Her mother said, "Oh, Edgar, I am so happy that you are here. You're family."

Helen took a quick bite of meat to control her urge to correct her mother. Legally, he was not family anymore, and under no circumstance would Helen consider him as such.

"Maybe you can talk some sense into Helen," her mother continued. "A day doesn't go by that I haven't worried myself sick about the dangers where Helen works."

Her father said, "What your mother is trying to say is, the shipyard is a dangerous place to work."

"Yes," her mother said. "Haven't we suffered enough with your brother's death? I can't bear to lose you, too."

The body falling flashed through Helen's mind. Yes, it was a dangerous place to work. However, she did not intend to quit her job. Her mother was the last person she would tell about the murder.

"Can't we talk about something fun now?" Amy asked.

Edgar turned to Amy. "You and your mother coming home back home would be fun, wouldn't it?"

The walls appeared to be moving in on Helen. She was trapped in a prison built by other people's expectations for who she was supposed to be. Anger and exhaustion smothered her. To combat her feeling of suffocation, she concentrated on the large flowered wallpaper, tried to figure out if the flowers were a poor imitation of chrysanthemums or an artist's invention. It was impossible to change the ambiance. Her brother Phillip's ghost sucked the air out of the room and Edgar's presence stung like salt in an open wound.

"What's for dessert, Grandma?" Amy said.

"I baked your favorite cookies. Eat your vegetables so you can have them."

Helen didn't like her mother bribing Amy, but didn't say anything.

Edgar waited until he had everyone's attention before saying, "Helen, you've accomplished a lot working in the shipyard. I'm proud of you."

She thanked him coolly. She didn't care if he was proud or not.

He reached over and clutched her hand with his fingers. "Now, it's time for you and Amy to come home."

Helen pushed her fingernails into the palm of his hand.

He drew it back but didn't say anything.

Helen helped Amy out of her chair. "Why don't you go play with Sam in the kitchen until we have dessert?"

When the swinging door closed, Helen said to her parents in a low voice, "You know why I left him. I had no choice."

"Why?" her father asked.

"You didn't tell him?" she asked her mother, who shrugged. Without waiting for an answer, Helen told her father about Edgar's affair, rushing through the story before Edgar could cut her off.

"Honey," her mother said. "You don't want to be a divorcée. There must be some way you could make this work."

Her father sprung out of his chair, squeezed his hand into a fist and leaned over Edgar. "You son of a...gun."

"Lloyd. What on earth are you doing?" her mother asked.

"I think Edgar should leave," he said, his voice thick with hate.

"You are the host. Why are you acting so rude? I don't even know you."

Helen scraped her chair back and ran up the stairs to her bedroom.

She looked around the room at the dotted Swiss bedspread and curtains. Straw hats, to match the ones on the wallpaper, tied the curtains back. A dressing table made of orange crates and pink ruffled skirts stood against one wall and a maple desk against another. She had outgrown this room long ago, and yet she only now recognized that it was elegant in a way that she had never realized when she had lived in it. She was embarrassed to realize she was spoiled, raised with all the luxuries that so many girls never had. She'd taken it all for granted when she lived here, and yet, had she been happy?

On her desk, Helen noticed *The Saturday Evening Post*, May 29, 1943, with the Norman Rockwell painting of Rosie the Riveter on the cover. Helen had left the magazine during those four days after she and Amy came to Portland and stayed with her mother while her father was in Washington and her apartment at Vanport wasn't quite ready.

She grabbed the magazine and climbed out her window to sit on the roof over the side porch, as she had done many times growing up, to calm her anger. Moonlight tinted Rosie's nail polish and lipstick red cellophane. Helen looked down at the pavement below and wondered, if she jumped, whether her shattered bones would create the feeling their soldiers had when they came ashore on that concave beach and German bullets devoured them like killer bees.

Helen observed the magazine cover. A pair of goggles pushed back Rosie's red curly hair. Her eyes were half closed. Her nose was pert, her face tilted. Smudges of oil or dirt covered parts of her muscular arms, one hand holding a ham sandwich. She wore bright red lipstick and nail polish. A riveting tool lay across her lap, the cord circling her thick, coverall-clad legs all the way down to her pennyloafers, with which she stomped a swastika on a copy of *Mein Kampf*. Helen took comfort that Rosie was feminine and capable of doing a man's job. She felt as though the two of them had a conversation and decided that Helen didn't need this roof anymore. And she didn't need her parents' approval. She could make her own decisions.

Yes, it was time to take Amy back to their new home where Helen had struggled to achieve a productive life for them. She took *The Saturday Evening Post* and rushed down the stairs. The scent of pure butter called up her memory of coming home from school and having cookies that her mother had just baked. She wavered for a second. Maybe she should let Amy stay for just one night. Helen looked at Edgar, her mother and her father's empty seat. She would not subject Amy to any more conflict.

She took a cookie, put the magazine in her purse and told Amy they had to leave.

"I want to stay," Amy said.

Helen's mother pleaded, "Let her spend the night."

Helen took the wrapped cookies that her mother had prepared for Amy, and said, "What will your friends say if you are not at school tomorrow?"

"Okie dokie," Amy said as she stood up and slipped her hand into Helen's palm.

Chapter Three

After a fitful night's sleep, Helen woke up. Her jaws ached from grinding her teeth. Through the edges of the blackout blinds, she saw daylight. The clock on her bedside table showed seven o'clock. She had forgotten to set the alarm and had overslept half an hour. Amy sat on the floor surrounded by her blocks and coloring books.

Helen sprung out of bed and pulled the blinds up. Helen disliked the blinds intensely. They cast a dark hue on the room like an evil spirit and were difficult to pull up and down. All defense plant areas, including the housing that was so close to the shipyard, were required to use such precautions.

She threw the print quilt over her bedding and picked out Amy's dress and sweater, which she spread on her bed. Helen slid into her coveralls and work shirt as she headed for the kitchen area. When she had squeezed the orange juice and poured their cereal, she called to Amy.

"I'm busy packing my school bag," Amy replied.

Helen took three steps to the bedroom they were forced to share. Dolls, coloring books, crayons, and a rubber ball were spread over the bed. The rest of Amy's toys were on the floor next to her empty toy basket and had rumpled the throw rug.

"Get dressed this minute," she ordered her daughter.

Amy pinched her lips, ready to cry.

"Never mind," Helen said, with a sigh of resignation, as she pulled off Amy's pajamas.

Once she was dressed, Amy sat in her youth chair and stared at her cereal bowl. "I want Crumbles," she said petulantly.

Helen took some milk from the refrigerator. "You said you don't like those anymore. You like to hear the Rice Krispies pop when I pour the milk."

"I want Crumbles." Amy rubbed her eyes and cried.

This wasn't fair to Amy. Helen had been selfish to expect her to adapt to this new environment. Every morning they had to leave early, so that Helen could get Amy settled into school and still arrive at work on time for her shift. They were always rushing. Helen needed to control her impatience. She poured the Crumbles into a plastic container. This would be enough breakfast because Amy would have a healthy lunch prepared by the cooks at the childcare center.

"Here, you can eat these on the way like a walking picnic."

Amy laughed but Helen hadn't recovered from the case of doubts that had seized her over bringing Amy to Vanport. When they arrived at school, Amy saw her friends and skipped down the hall to join them. But her happiness didn't compare to the sheer joy she had displayed with Edgar the night before.

When Helen got off the bus, rain pummeled her face and exuded a rotten-egg mold odor after it hit the ground. She walked past the plating shop and the administration building on her way to the ship.

Helen noticed Charlotte, her blond hair curling from the rain, walking near her, and decided this was a good opportunity to question Charlotte in hopes of ending the doubts that still plagued Helen over whether she had done the right thing when she had identified Charlotte as the lone person on the deck the day of the murder.

"Did you know Erich?" Helen said, trying to see if Charlotte's expression changed when she heard the sound of his name.

"That loudmouth?" Charlotte didn't seem guilty, but maybe she was good at hiding her emotions. "Everyone knew him."

"Who do you think killed him?"

"He was a nasty person. I bet there are a hundred people who would've loved to get rid of him."

"We don't go around killing unpleasant people," Helen said, taken aback by Charlotte's response.

"Obviously, someone did. He was really hard on his workers, especially the women. One time I saw him drop his hat on the deck and stomp on it. Then he screamed at a woman, told her that from then on, he would make her work so hard she would quit."

"Who was it?" Helen asked, trying to conceal the excitement in her voice.

"I don't know. He treated all the women like that." Charlotte's face flushed. Her voice rose with anger. "He called my husband a slant-eyed chink and asked if my children had slant-eyes. He said all the slant-eyes are behind barbed wire where they belong."

"Your whole family is in the internment camp?" Helen asked, feeling a wash of pity for Charlotte, regardless of whether or not she was guilty. She had read about the camps in the *Oregonian* and thought the way the government herded the Japanese away from their homes and possessions was a travesty. So many innocent people were treated like criminals.

"I just told you this to show how rude Erich was," Charlotte said awkwardly, obviously not wanting to continue a personal discussion about her family and the war.

Helen was disappointed that Charlotte closed the conversation, but her tone of voice was firm. Helen knew she had to drop the subject.

A worker bumped Helen in the side, which propelled her against Charlotte. Their shoulders collided, faces almost touching. Helen looked down at the ground. She had betrayed this poor, brave woman. She couldn't think of anything worse than being separated from a child. Charlotte was a mother. She couldn't imagine a mother killing a man and then pushing him overboard. Even if Charlotte was rightfully mad at Erich, she had other, bigger problems to worry about. Would she have told Helen about Erich's mean comments, would she have said how much she disliked him, if she had done anything criminal that she needed to cover up?

When they reached the ship, Helen was so worried about having incriminated Charlotte that she walked up the narrow steps without hesitation. She continued straight to the bow where she had been welding steel plates. Charlotte had already climbed up to her station at the smoke pipe above the deckhouse.

Helen plugged in her electrode holder and tried to blot out all other thoughts besides the task in front of her. She began welding the two sheets of steel together as reinforcement for the wooden hull. She had hoped to get information to clear her suspicion about Charlotte. Instead she got a motive. With her children and husband interned, Erich's derogatory remarks about them might have pushed her too far.

Helen realized her electrode was in mid-air and forced herself to weld the rest of the seam.

"Hey, slowpoke, you're holdin' us other folks up. This ain't one of your tea parties."

She recognized Betty's voice and turned to look at her. Betty was older than most of the workers. She and her husband had earned money for most of their lives by picking fruit and as tenant farmers. They both worked at the yard now. She looked to be in her late fifties. Wrinkles had formed on her forehead and around her mouth. She had large eyes and freckled cheeks. Still, she would be more attractive if she lost some weight. Her big stomach and her hips pushed against her pants. Her biceps were firm, probably from picking fruit.

Before she started working here, someone like Betty would probably have disgusted Helen. But Helen had seen many women as old and as poor as Betty at the shipyard and they interested her. Sometimes she let thoughts of them overwhelm her. What would it be like to try to find work from day to day, not knowing if you could buy food or would go hungry?

Helen told Betty she was sorry, though, in her own opinion, she was doing just fine.

"Sorry won't cut it," Betty said with authority that infuriated Helen.

She stood up for herself. "I'm right on schedule."

"You rich people always think you're right," Betty said like a smart-aleck kid.

"That was a terrible thing to say," Charlotte said, appearing around the corner.

Helen contrasted her cheerful smile to Betty's sour expression.

"Why you sticking up for her?" Betty directed her defiance at Charlotte. "She's divorced, you know. People like her ain't supposed to do that."

Charlotte refused to let go. "Where'd you get that idea?"

"You don't have to play dumb with me. You know damn well she is only working here because she thinks we ain't good enough to judge her."

"You can't blame Helen for your hard times," Charlotte scolded.

"Rich people need someone to toughen 'em up."

Charlotte frowned at Betty. "You sound like a lead electrician with your bossy attitude."

"Fat chance. If they did offer me the job, I wouldn't take it. More work and less pay than the lead men get, only because I'm a woman."

Helen felt as limp as the wilted lettuce in the victory garden she and Amy had planted. How could she think that someone as nice as Charlotte would kill anyone? What if Helen had ruined her life with mistaken accusations?

Chapter Four

At the end of the day, exhausted by work and overcome by the conflicting tides of emotions that kept sweeping over her, Helen ran all the way to the bus stop and stepped inside just before the doors closed and the driver pulled away from the curb. The motor whooshed and rumbled, sending thick fumes of burnt gasoline through the bus. She sat down next to a man who exuded the scent of whiskey. He looked like the men she had seen on Burnside Street, drinking wine, the ones her father said had messed up their lives instead of doing a hard day's work.

She glanced up and caught sight of Charlotte and Roxanne walking together down the aisle. Helen looked out the window so she wouldn't have to talk to them until she had cleared her doubts about Charlotte. Outside the window, she saw the FBI man, who had been consulting with the sheriff, walking along the pavement, swinging one arm and holding a briefcase in his other hand. Helen jumped out of her seat and the motion of the moving bus almost knocked her down. Her heart beat so hard that swallowing was impossible. Grasping the seatback in front of her, she stood again and shouted, "Stop the bus!"

"What the hell?" the driver said.

"Stop. This is an emergency," Helen insisted, embarrassed by the fact that Roxanne and Charlotte, who were now seated behind her, had no doubt seen her stumble. They must have been wondering why she was acting so strangely. She hoped they were too absorbed in whatever they were talking about to pay her much attention.

Brakes squealed. The motor shook to a stop. A man yelled, "Hey, Lady, you nuts?" and another person said, "Who made you boss?"

"Helen, what's wrong?" Charlotte said. Apparently she had seen everything.

"I forgot something. I'll take the next bus," Helen stammered, wondering if it was obvious that she was lying.

"It can't be that important," Roxanne said.

Rather than responding, she dashed off the bus, ducked behind a row of cars and walked forward, waiting for the bus to drive out of sight. It appeared to be moving in slow motion. Would she miss the FBI man?

Helen heard the click of shoes hitting pavement. Be patient, she told herself. Maybe this was a stupid idea in the first place. Finally the bus chugged ahead, roaring like a deep sigh. Helen cut between a rusty Studebaker and a Desoto and called to the officer.

"Agent Miller," she said, straining her vocal chords.

He turned and raised his brows above blue eyes. Having seen him only from a distance, Helen was impressed with his appearance. He was tall, broad-shouldered and had blond hair. His eyes seemed to probe her as though he could see inside her mind.

"My name is Dan."

"I need to talk to you about a suspect," she said.

"You work here?" he asked, sounding surprised.

Helen nodded. "I saw you earlier on the ship where I weld."

"It's amazing to me. Someone as small as you can climb up and down the rigging every day, not to mention holding the tool steady."

Inwardly Helen fumed at the comment he'd probably intended to be a compliment. Why did everyone treat her like a child? She couldn't do anything to make herself grow taller, but she vowed to do chin-ups on the metal clothesline poles outside the apartment building to build her muscles like Rosie's. She decided to push his remark out of her mind.

"I am concerned that I may have given the sheriff the wrong information." Helen glanced at him but couldn't read what he thought of her statement. She continued, "I saw someone on the ship right after the man fell. I think I gave a false identification."

"Why don't we go down to FBI Headquarters," he suggested, looking interested to learn more about whatever she had to tell him.

"I have to pick my daughter up at the Vanport nursery." Some part of her hoped that he wouldn't assume that just because she had a daughter, she was also happily married.

"I'll drive you there," he said, which she took as a good sign.

They walked along the parking lot, past Studebakers, Fords, and an old LaSalle, past a few buses, to a black Ford sedan. Dan opened the passenger-side door and Helen stepped on the running board and into the front seat while he found his way to the driver's seat. The scent of new upholstery blended with the sandalwood of his aftershave.

"I told the sheriff that I thought the person I saw was Charlotte Yamamoto," she began. "But I regret that I identified her because there was a considerable distance between us and I only saw the figure for a second and not its face. After thinking about it more, I'm almost sure it couldn't have been Charlotte."

He smiled, without taking his eyes off the road, and Helen immediately felt that he understood her feelings. He said, "You did the right thing by telling what you could. Now you must trust that the authorities examine all leads they receive, including research, fingerprints, and meticulous examination of the deceased. As it turns out, the sheriff shared that information with me. Something about her walk, he said you recognized."

"Did the two of you have a good laugh?"

Dan was stopped at an intersection. He looked at her. "Of course not."

"I guess he already had his fun when he interviewed me earlier."

"We all have different ways of interviewing."

Helen realized, regretfully, that they were already on Denver Street, a few blocks from Amy's school, and rushed to say, "I know he didn't take what I said very seriously, but I learned something else from Charlotte later on. Erich made fun of her husband and children, for being Japanese. That would give her a motive, too."

"I'm interested in your interpretation."

She was being pulled deeper into the role of witness, but if she wanted to be taken seriously, she had no choice but to reveal everything that she knew. Besides, a man had died. It was her duty to be honest, to put morality above a new and uncertain friendship. "Her family is in an internment camp and Erich taunted her. He could have hit a nerve, though I don't think she would have told me this if she were guilty."

"That's possible," Dan agreed. "As I said, we will weigh your information with the coroner's report and our lab results from the murder scene."

Helen liked that he was taking her—her opinions, what she had to say on this most serious of matters—seriously.

Other cars whizzed by. Helen felt as though they floated around her. How did she ever get into this situation? Though Charlotte was a friend, Helen had to admit that she felt better after telling Dan about her suspicions.

Dan parked his car in front of the child center. He took a card from his pocket. "Please call me if you think of anything else."

She tensed her hand to stop it from shaking as she took the card. "Thanks for the ride."

"I'll speak to you soon even if I don't have any more questions."

Her pulse tapped her breastplate. She smiled at him. "I'll be waiting."

Waiting. That must have made a great impression. Helen found Amy swinging in the play yard with other children. Her laughter was a melody to Helen. The number of children there assured her that, rather than being late, she had arrived before the mothers on the bus did.

As soon as she and Amy returned to their apartment, Helen suggested they work in the victory garden, to make up for her impatience with Amy that morning. Helen filled the watering can a third of the way, making sure it was not too heavy for Amy. Though the hoe and rake were child-size, they were taller than Amy. Helen held the watering can while Amy dragged her rake and hoe to the garden, a tiny dirt patch next to the outside wall of the apartment building. Together, they raked the dirt before watering the plants.

"Look, Mommy, a tomato." Amy pointed to the slightly green vegetable. "Can we have it for dinner? Can we?"

"Absolutely." Though the tomato was not quite ripe, Helen reached down and picked it from the plant. She couldn't resist Amy's excitement.

Helen had tucked Amy into bed when the telephone rang. Did she dare think it was Dan? When she answered, Edgar's harsh voice came through the earpiece.

"Helen?"

Hearing him say her name made Helen wince. She thought it ironic that Edgar had used his influence and money to have a telephone installed so he could talk to Amy, and she had been enjoying it until that moment. Since there were no phones in the apartments it was quite an achievement. Now, however, with him on the other end of the line, it just reminded her that he still had control over her life. It also brought her back to the days when her mother would argue for her right to something that others didn't have. Helen had worked so hard to get away, and she shouldn't still be living with privileges afforded by Edgar and his dubious connections.

She could see him sprawled out on the tweed chair and ottoman in the mahogany-paneled den, moping over their framed wedding picture. "What do you want, Edgar?"

"I'm calling from the hotel." The rattle of ice in a glass imitated his self-important voice. He must have brought liquor with him from home, though she wouldn't put it past him to finagle a state liquor license. Nothing as trivial as Oregon being a dry state would stop him.

"You're still here?"

He barely let her finish her question. "I'm going to take Amy home with me now instead of in August."

"Absolutely not. Our custody agreement gives you the month in August."

"That's what you think." Edgar often used that phrase when he had one of his dreadful plans, right before he pulled the rug out from under her.

"I'm sorry I had to leave you," Helen said, straining to be nice to Edgar.

He took a deep breath and talked nonstop. "No, you aren't. We had a nice life, with all the luxuries. You were wrong, wrong to take Amy away. Let me talk to her."

Helen sighed. "She's asleep."

"You and I need to talk. I'll come by tomorrow," Edgar said without pausing.

She pictured stuffing cotton into his mouth. "Listen to me, Edgar, don't come here and don't call again. I'm going to hang up now." The dial tone buzzing in her ear, Helen took deep breaths and exhaled to expel her anger. She would have loved to soak in a tub to wash off the phone conversation, but since the tiny bathroom had only a shower, she settled for that. The water splashed on her face, ran down her body to the tile, and formed rivulets twirling around the drain. She imagined Edgar's words following the water.

As soon as she nestled under her sheet, the neighbors' voices started the same way they did most nights. The man slurred his words in a husky voice: "Shut up, whore," followed by language Helen had never heard before she came to Vanport. She could put up with that and even the noisy drinking and crying babies. But the frequent fires—a result of using their stoves as heaters—highlighted by constant fire-engine sirens, scared her enough to consider finding another place to live. Then she would have to find a babysitter for Amy, because after a longer drive she wouldn't have time to drop Amy off at the preschool in Vanport. Wanting to go to sleep with something nice in her head, she clapped her hands over her ears, blotted out all thoughts about Edgar, and pictured Dan in bathing trunks, his muscular body suntanned. This was no way to feel about an FBI man working on the murder case in which she was a witness.

Chapter Five

The lunchroom smelled of smoke and peanut butter. Helen sat with the same women that she did every day, crowded around the small primitive table. Embarrassment burned Helen's cheeks when Charlotte sat next to her. Looking at the well-kept, kind and considerate woman beside her, she was more certain than ever that Charlotte was obviously not a killer.

Helen asked herself what she had done, why she had turned her accusations on this poor woman whose family had been taken from her. Of course, she had no choice. She worked in a defense factory and it was her responsibility to report what she had seen. And it would surely amount to nothing, since Charlotte had clearly committed no crime.

The sound of shoes tapping linoleum, of chairs scraping and voices shouting, grew louder as more workers appeared. Roxanne sat across from Helen and Charlotte. She was tall and slender with large breasts accentuated by a tight-fitting pale blue sweater. She wore thick foundation and heavy mascara that had spread onto the skin beneath her eyes like a shadow, making her look exhausted.

Charlotte finished her sandwich and took a puff from her Lucky Strike cigarette, which she held between her index and middle fingers, and exhaled slowly while surveying Roxanne. "You shouldn't wear a sweater, it's dangerous. Don't you have a smock or something to wear in the yard? There's so much debris, not to mention the times you are on the ships."

"That's what Erich told me, though I knew he liked me in sweaters," Roxanne said. She patted her eyes with a handkerchief. "I can't believe he's dead."

Helen noticed that Roxanne seemed to be staring at Charlotte and studying how she held her cigarette. Roxanne shaped her mouth like Charlotte, as though she, too, were smoking.

"Would you like a smoke?" Charlotte said, obviously noticing the same thing.

Roxanne blushed and nodded. She held the cigarette between her fingers, lit it, inhaled, and blew out the smoke identical to the way Charlotte had done. At first Helen thought she was making fun of Charlotte, but Roxanne's face said worship.

"Where'd you guys go?" Betty said as she approached the table, sat down, and took a Spam sandwich out of her lunchbox.

Charlotte glanced at Helen and shrugged her shoulders. Helen smiled like a friend. Some friend. She had betrayed Charlotte.

"We're talking about Erich," Roxanne said, taking a bite of carrot.

"I ain't surprised someone killed him," Betty said. "He was nastier than a rabid hound. He should'a been nicer to us. He screamed all the time."

Roxanne blushed. "He was nice to me."

Betty leaned across the table. "You told me he used you."

"I never said that." Roxanne pushed her lips out like a pouting child. "We were in love and I'm carrying his baby," she blurted out, looking at them expectantly as she awaited their reactions.

"How could you? He's married," Charlotte said, her voice full of disgust.

"He was separated. They were going to get a divorce."

"That's what they all say," Betty said. "You going to give the kid away?"

Roxanne took two gigantic capsules from a pill bottle and swallowed them with water. "Absolutely not. The baby will be a part of Erich. And I'm going to take acting lessons so I can support my baby."

Helen felt disgusted. She had thought that Roxanne was nice— not necessarily the smartest woman in the shipyard, but sweet. She couldn't believe that Roxanne wasn't even trying to hide the fact that she was pregnant. In fact, she wanted everyone to see she was taking pills, vitamins no doubt. It would be bad enough when she started showing and would lose her job, but why broadcast it early? She could be fired and be a single mother without money, raising a baby out of wedlock.

"Don't get your hopes up," Charlotte said. "Hollywood is a tough place to succeed."

"Don't I know it." Roxanne took a compact from her purse and powdered her face. "My poor momma tried out for every bit part and never saw a camera."

"Did you live there?" Helen asked, hoping to understand Roxanne better by trying to coax more of her personal story out of her.

"All my life. My daddy did all the dangerous stunts for the stars."

"Well, a bunch of lessons ain't going to guarantee you can support a child," Betty said. "Besides, why would you want Erich's kid? He'd probably be a loser, too."

"Why are you so angry about Erich?" Helen asked Betty, suddenly wondering whether Betty too might have had a special reason to dislike him, to wish him gone. "A lot of men here are rude to women."

Betty's sour face loomed at Helen from across the table. "I don't like mean people."

Helen almost choked in her effort to avoid asking Betty if she disliked herself. The chorus of metal lunchboxes closing reminded her lunchtime had ended. Her role as a witness to Erich's murder had hovered over the table like an uninvited guest. She took an apple, which she would eat on the way to the ship, and closed her box.

As Charlotte walked to the exit, the sight of her ballerina walk, and the back of her coveralls, took Helen back to the murder scene. She began to shake.

"You all right?" Betty said.

"Just tired," Helen said, which was true.

They caught up with Charlotte and Roxanne and walked toward the ship. Helen resented being stuck walking beside Betty. Roxanne hardly looked at them. She walked slightly behind Charlotte and imitated her ballerina walk precisely. Helen wondered why Roxanne wanted to be exactly like Charlotte. The poor girl probably saw Charlotte as a woman of class and thought she could improve her own social standing if she imitated Charlotte.

A woman, definitely not a worker, distracted Helen by taking exaggerated steps around the group, her mouth turned down in disgust. She wore a black-and-white-checked rayon crepe skirt and short-sleeved jacket with large shoulder pads and a large lace collar and black patent leather platform pumps with high heels. She had straight blond hair down to her shoulders, which made her seem old fashioned since curls were in style. She squared her shoulders, making the pads overpower her thin body.

After the woman walked away, Betty said, "That's Erich's wife."

Roxanne took small steps, her head bent toward the ground. Helen felt sorry for her, even if she had done something shameful, and tried to diffuse the situation but couldn't think of anything funny to say. The best Helen could do was to make an observation. "She looks out of place here."

Roxanne rewarded her with a smile, while Betty acted as though she hadn't heard her and Charlotte said, "She probably came to get his things."

"Why didn't you say something to her?" Betty asked.

Charlotte ignored her.

Their exchange troubled Helen. "You know that woman?" she asked Charlotte.

Betty spoke before Charlotte could answer. "Didn't she buy your doll shop?"

"You're really being nosy," Charlotte said.

Helen was curious, too, and luckily Betty was willing to push. Helen didn't have to wait long for an answer.

"Why are you so secretive?" Betty asked. "Everyone knows the Japs had to sell everything."

Helen fought with herself. If she didn't say anything, Betty would pry out all the information she needed from Charlotte. Betty's eyes centered on Charlotte like a dog eyeing a steak. Her pleasure in goading the poor woman was more than Helen could stand. "Can't you take a hint, Betty? Charlotte doesn't want to talk about it."

"Geez. Stay out of it, rich girl."

Helen noticed that by that point Erich's widow was almost out of sight, the back of her checked suit fading in the distance. "I've got to go."

"Helen," Charlotte called to her. "What's with you? Have you gone bonkers?"

Helen ignored her and took long strides. Without taking her eyes off the black-and-white check, she followed the woman past the ships, across the grass, beyond the line of buses to a black Packard. A luxury car for the wife of a shipyard worker? When Helen got closer to her, she noticed her purse was more like a suitcase. As the widow approached, a chauffeur jumped out of the car and took the bundle from her.

A large shoe with a metal tip fell to the ground and an envelope flitted close by. *Evidence.* The word pummeled Helen's brain. She couldn't take her eyes off the letter. The chauffeur opened the door for the widow and picked up the shoe. Helen didn't have any more time. She rubbed the toe of her shoe on the cement and executed a fake fall, throwing herself on top of the letter. The throbbing in her knee was not fake. As she wrapped her arms around her shoulders, she scooted the letter into the bib of her coveralls.

The chauffeur ran over to Helen. "What the?"

Helen looked up at him. He was tall. His arms were larger than her waist, and muscular like a wrestler. Had he seen her take the letter? She cringed.

He towered over Helen and stared at her. "What the devil are you doing here?"

Afraid to stand up, Helen didn't know what to do. If the chauffeur had seen her take the letter, he could knock her over and, after killing her, take it back.

She felt moisture, obviously blood, running from her knee down her shin. The chauffeur hadn't budged, which made Helen lightheaded enough without looking at her injuries.

"Are you hurt?"

She sighed with relief and followed his gaze. Blood had seeped through her coveralls. Her knee and the palms of her hands burned. She didn't want him to continue observing her. Pain shot up her entire body as she pushed herself up. "Just embarrassed." *And petrified,* she thought.

"What are you doing here?" he asked.

"I work here and I was looking for a bus schedule. Have you seen one?"

The widow rolled down her window. "Joseph, let's go."

"You'd think they would have them posted here," Helen said before she hobbled toward the ship. She detoured to her locker and glanced around. No one was nearby. Did she dare read the letter now? She placed it inside her locker and stuck her head inside. Footsteps sounded. She eased her head out, slammed the metal door, and locked it. What kind of letter would Erich leave with his shipyard paraphernalia? She would have to wait to find out.

Chapter Six

The day's work completed, Helen was exhausted. With the added tension over Erich's murder, long hours of precise labor were almost unbearable. Her purse felt weighed down by the letter she had stolen from the widow. Helen hadn't planned to be a thief. If there were any other way to solve the mystery of Erich's death, she would have avoided breaking the law.

The crowd had already headed for the buses and she wouldn't have any privacy until after she got back to Vanport. She couldn't stop. If she missed the first bus, she would be late to pick up Amy.

After getting her at the child care center, she received the carton that contained their pre-cooked dinner from the nutrition center. It was braised beef and vegetables. The strong scent of aged beef and onions permeated the carton. Though the meal didn't excite Helen, she rarely had the energy to cook dinner.

"I don't want that dinner," Amy said. "The gravy is icky."

Helen took a deep breath. Her body ached with fatigue. "I'll make mashed potatoes to go with it. We'll go buy some at the store."

"Okie dokie. And some hot dogs."

"We'll see," Helen said, too tired to argue. She really didn't blame Amy. The meals of skimpy meat, drowned in gravy, had become boring. Before rationing, she had given Amy wieners often, because it was all she would eat. Lately, it didn't make sense to spend the same amount of red stamps on the sausage as for a small steak.

They stopped briefly at their apartment for Helen to pick up her cloth bag, which she had been using since the paper shortage became acute. She disliked carrying the bag, but paper was needed for manufacturing ammunition. She drove her Chevy to the shopping center.

The Groceteria was huge. The meat department alone was larger than an ice-skating rink. They walked past rows of canned vegetables and fruits. There was a long line waiting for the sugar. Helen decided not to wait and walked on past the flour and Betty Crocker cake mixes to the Cocomalt, which she put in her bag before moving on to more canned goods. The Hearts Delight asparagus tempted her, but the Del Monte applesauce that Amy loved cost twelve points, amusing since the item itself cost only sixteen cents. Helen stopped to check her ration book. She had seventy blue stamps left to last them until the end of the month. She took a can of the applesauce and some string beans and searched for marshmallows to go with the Cocomalt when Amy ran towards the meat counter.

Helen's mouth turned dry. Amy could get lost in the aisles, which were larger than bowling alleys. She chased Amy all the way to the glass case filled with wieners, almost bumping into Betty, the last person she wanted to see. Dealing with Amy was enough; she didn't need to cope with this sour woman. Luckily, Betty was concentrating on her ration book.

"I want a hot dog for dinner," Amy said, her lips puckered, ready to cry.

Helen controlled her impatience. "We have the meat. I'll take the gravy off."

"Hot dog!" Amy cried.

Betty glanced at them and turned back to look at her stamps, which pleased Helen because this was none of Betty's business. Helen took Amy by the hand and dragged her towards the front of the grocery. Through the door, Helen saw a man step out of a Rolls Royce. Even before he came closer she identified him as Edgar. Only he would wear a dark suit, imported white shirt, and dark tie to a grocery store, unlike most of the shoppers who wore rain jackets and boots or saddle shoes.

"Let's go buy some wieners," Helen said, already turning around. She ran to keep up with Amy, who was skipping back to the meat counter. By the time Helen reached Amy, her nose was pressed against the glass case. Helen prayed that Edgar wouldn't see them. No such luck. He intruded between Amy and Helen. She wondered what laws he had broken to get enough gas ration stamps to drive all the way here.

"I didn't know you drove your car from California," she said accusingly.

His eyes rested on Amy. "It's impossible to get reservations on an airplane or train."

Helen shivered. He had followed them here. Had he been watching them since he had arrived in town yesterday? Or had he been in town and stalking her longer? Apparently, he wanted her to fail at her job and her quest for independence.

"Daddy!" Amy hugged him. "You going to stay in Oregon?"

"No, Pumpkin, I'm going to take you back to California with me now." He kept looking at Amy as though Helen weren't there.

"Mommy, too?"

"If she wants to," he said, still ignoring Helen.

Rage choked her. She tried to smile but her throat was dry and she could barely squeeze out a few words. "Not Amy. Not me." She had planned to take some time off in August. By then she would have some days coming so she could travel to California and check on Amy.

"We'll see about that," Edgar said, frowning at Helen's workclothes as though she were the one out of place. "I'm entitled to my month and Amy wants to come." He put his arm around Amy's shoulder. "Don't you, Pumpkin?"

Out of the corner of her eye, Helen saw Betty, a wrapped package of meat in hand, staring at Edgar. How long had she been watching? Helen lowered her voice. "That's right. In August."

Edgar's ears turned crimson. "If you don't have her ready to leave with me by tomorrow, I'm going to take you to court and poke holes in your quickie divorce."

"I wouldn't try that if I were you." Helen knew Edgar was impossible to live with, knew he had lied and cheated, both in love and in business, to get what he wanted, with no consideration for whom he might hurt, so this latest show of ruthlessness didn't surprise her. She would like to think that she worked at the shipyard only to help the war effort and honor her brother. And she did feel good about her work there. But the necessity or having her own money, separate and secret from Edgar, and insuring that Amy was not exposed to his dishonesty: this was her main goal. Earning her own money made Helen feel strong. She deserved to be taken seriously. But she was also afraid of what he could pull off, with his unscrupulous, self-serving ways.

Edgar continued his one-sided conversation. "Oh, I will, and after I prove that our divorce is not legal, I will get full custody of Amy."

She would have loved to say: just try it. I have enough money to hire a sharp lawyer. She said, "If you ever try to sue for custody, I'll report you to the government for selling tires on the black market." Helen clutched her bag, grabbed Amy's hand, and rushed over to the other side of the store.

Helen's meeting with Edgar caused her to want Dan's company. She told herself that she was only going to call Dan because she needed to voice her suspicions about Roxanne. She hadn't known him that long. Did she dare call him in the evening? The encounter with Edgar made her long for someone who made her feel appreciated. Vivid images of Dan's spontaneous smile, his deep blue eyes, and the feel of his strong shoulders taunted her.

Chapter Seven

When Helen woke up the next morning, she realized that with all of the chaos at the grocery, she hadn't read the letter of Erich's that had tumbled from the widow's purse. Before she fixed breakfast she read the letter:

> *You still owe me $3,000.00 per our purchase agreement. If I do not receive it by end of month, I will contact my lawyer.*

Was this letter from Charlotte? Now she had more to tell Dan. Helen called in sick. Then she picked up the receiver again, intending to call Dan, but slammed it back in the cradle. She had to call him. She had to tell him her new suspicions regarding Roxanne. Why was she so reticent? Maybe it frightened her that she needed Dan to escape Edgar—one man to get away from another. She dialed Dan's number again. He seemed happy to hear from her, which she took as encouragement.

"I have some information on another suspect in the killing," she said. "I called in sick today."

"Come to my office. We can go out to lunch afterwards."

His invitation gave her courage. "Sounds good to me," she said, hoping she didn't sound too eager.

That was so easy that Helen began to have doubts. If he were interested in her, she would have to put the brakes on. She shouldn't jump into another relationship so fast. She had made a mistake to marry Edgar, which made her mistrust her own judgment. How could she know if Dan was different?

At first, she had truly loved Edgar—or had she? Pictures of Edgar and her at formal balls showed a handsome couple, smiling happily. She wore a black strapless gown and he wore a tuxedo with a custom-made pleated shirt. Thinking about the picture, she remembered their teeth, overly white and forming obviously staged smiles. At the time, she believed that she was happy. Her life was filled with dinner parties, bridge games, luncheons, and volunteer work. Filled, but not full. Occasionally, a strange numbness poked her stomach. At first, she ignored it. But the emptiness prevailed. Maybe it was because Edgar was away on business or worked long hours, or was in bed with one of his harlots, as she had verified before leaving him. She considered going back to school.

Then she was pregnant, and preoccupied by a whirlwind of baby showers and getting the nursery ready. Amy was a joy. Helen threw herself into being a good mother and ignored the signs of Edgar's dishonesty when his warehouse filled with new tires each time he traveled to Canada. How dare he take rubber that sailors needed for life vests and lifeboats? A year after the Japanese had attacked Pearl Harbor, the draft board called up men with children and Edgar found a doctor to write a letter that he had asthma, though Helen had never seen any symptoms. Soon she had to face the fact that her husband was a dishonorable man.

Helen had to take Amy to school. When she returned, she turned on her Emerson Victory radio. The Andrews sisters were singing "Don't Sit Under the Apple Tree." She took a quick shower, set her hair in pin curls, and applied some Ann Barton leg make-up, which she smoothed with cotton balls. The procedure was a nuisance, but silk worms grown in Japan were, of course, off-limits and all the nylon, a synthetic that could have been manufactured as stockings, went to make parachutes for the Air Force.

While her legs dried, she powdered her face, rubbed some rouge into her cheeks, and brushed her hair into loose curls. She slipped into a dirndl skirt, peasant blouse, and white sandals. It was a joy not to wear the bulky coveralls and heavy oxfords. This didn't mean that she wasn't proud to accomplish the difficult labor for her country, nor that she didn't wear the coveralls with pride like Rosie the Riveter. It just felt good to be truly feminine this one time, especially when she would see Dan.

The wheels of her Chevy rumbled across the Burnside Bridge. She took the Washington exit, turned left on third, and continued on to Main Street, where she parked across the street from the Solomon Building Courthouse. Sun had poked through the clouds and highlighted the large building of gray sandstone. She walked up the steps and stopped in front of the entrance.

She noticed her hands were shaking. To calm herself, she concentrated on the bronze Art-Deco doors. Though beautiful, they did not distract her. Thoughts pounded her head while she walked through the marble entry but flitted away inside the lobby, where she was overwhelmed by the cherry and mahogany wood and cast-bronze friezes, grilles, geometric shapes, and floral designs. In the post office, the mailboxes were marked with cast-metal letters in black glass. Once she reached the elevator Helen's doubts returned. Dan had appeared to be happy to hear from her. That didn't make this any easier. The weight of being a witness hung on her like a load of bricks. When she found the FBI offices on the fourth floor, a uniformed guard greeted her. She told him she had an appointment with Dan, and then paced back and forth in the hallway until a man older than Dan walked toward her and smiled.

"I have an appointment with Agent Miller," she said.

His smile disappeared. "He's held up. I'm the chief agent in charge. Why don't you come into my office? We can talk there."

Helen scanned the reception room and slipped into the first chair she saw, a Naugahyde seat on a steel frame. "I'll wait." She watched the man walk away and let out a deep breath of relief. She had forgotten her worries that Dan would dismiss her observation of Roxanne.

A few minutes later, Dan stood above her. He wore a blue shirt and a tie loosened around the collar. She had to control her excitement at seeing him. His broad smile revealed that he was happy to see her, too. He led her to a small cubicle, crowded with a filing cabinet, two stiff chairs, and a desk that housed a Remington typewriter and piles of papers. Dan nodded for Helen to sit on one of the chairs while he sat across from her.

The words spilled out of her mouth. "I wanted to tell you about another suspect: Roxanne Cranston. She is a secretary in Administration."

"How do you connect her to the murder?" His interest appeared to be sincere.

"She has imitated Charlotte's walk," Helen said, fearing Dan would consider her information trivial. "At first, I though it was a strange form of admiration. I just happened to notice it, because it was so pronounced. Then I realized I could have seen Roxanne walking on the ship instead of Charlotte. I was too far away to see the woman's face."

Dan shuffled through some papers on his desk. "Another ballerina?"

Helen nodded, though she smarted from his apparent disinterest. He didn't even write the name down. Had he already made up his mind that Charlotte was guilty? The note Helen wanted to show him would verify his opinion. Whatever he would conclude, Helen had to be neutral. She reached in her purse, pulled out the envelope and handed it to him.

After Dan read the note, he said, "This certainly gives Charlotte a motive and fits in with the twist in our case." Dan said. "After all, she did own the doll shop at one time and now information about our ships is slipping out to our enemies. Apparently the doll shop is connected to the leak."

"But she doesn't own it anymore," Helen said, refusing to believe that Charlotte would be a spy.

"Have you seen any strangers loitering around the ship?"

"I don't think so," Helen said, taken aback by his question.

"Keep your eyes open. We've been alerted about a Japanese spy ring."

"Spies?" Helen said, unable to refrain from interrupting him.

He took a file from his cabinet and scanned a page. "Snitches wander around the shipyard and listen for conversations about ship repairs or ship itinerary." Dan handed Helen an envelope.

She surveyed the address. "Buenos Aires. It sounds exotic."

"Exotic?" Dan laughed. "I guess it is. I've been working at this job too long."

His laugh was contagious and Helen regretted that she had to turn back to the investigation. "The return address was in Seattle, but the letter was returned to sender. What was it doing in Portland?"

"Our bureau in Washington suspected it was connected to the spying in Oregon. We're still working on that."

Helen reached in for the letter and removed it. It reminded her of a scavenger hunt where you gather bits and pieces and someone holds all the right items. Not her. She felt totally confused. At first the letter read like a verbose woman writing to a friend.

I just secured a lovely Siamese Temple Dancer. It had been damaged, that is tore in the middle. But it is now repaired and I like it very much. I could not get a mate for this Siam dancer, so I am redressing just a small plain ordinary doll into a second Siam doll...

"It's a code," Dan explained. "The dolls represent ships and their schedules. When our crew analyzed it, they discerned that the types of dolls represented the type of ships that would be completed or repaired." He pointed to the letter. "For example, the reference to the *Siam dancer* means that a once-damaged ship would be returning. The other doll refers to the second ship, which has recently been constructed and will go into service against Japan."

To protect Americans, Helen knew she was obligated to report any unusual actions she noticed, but she needed to express her doubts, too. "I can't imagine Charlotte being involved in espionage."

Dan perused the pages in his file again. "It would be perfectly normal for her to be angry with our government for putting her family behind barbed wire. Of course, we are looking into all the suspects."

It was difficult for Helen to concentrate on new details because she was still thinking about Edgar's threats, which she couldn't dismiss. She had to say something. "I'll be observant."

Dan seemed to scrutinize her, a frown on his face. "Please don't worry about this. We have a handle on the investigation and will be vigilant."

Helen felt moisture in her eyes and strained to control her emotion. "I'm sorry. It's not the investigation that's worrying me. It's Edgar, my husband."

"Your husband?" Dan asked, rolling his chair back.

We're divorced," Helen said quickly to counter what she thought was disappointment in his question. She told Dan about dinner at her parents' house, and the scene at the market. "He threatened to sue for custody of Amy."

"He can't do that. You're her mother," Dan said, obviously angry.

Helen warmed to his support. "But I leave her at the child service center every day."

"To question that would be unpatriotic," Dan said, as though he, too, were being threatened. "No judge would go for that."

While Helen appreciated Dan's sensitivity, she struggled to squash her desire to depend on him. She looked behind Dan's desk at a framed document and around the room, which appeared to be growing smaller. She regretted having brought up the subject and rushed to end it. "I'll fight him. He sells black market tires and if I hear from him again, I'll report his crime."

Dan smiled. "I'll pretend I didn't hear that. Black market stuff isn't my department." Still smiling, he looked at his Longine watch and said, "Want to get a bite to eat?"

"I would love to," Helen said, embarrassed that she couldn't control her eagerness. He let her into his car, and together they drove over to Burnside Street and up to Henry Thiele's Restaurant. They both ordered roast beef and Thiele's famous potato pancakes, which were as good as she had remembered, though her mind was on other things than food. She enjoyed his company, and let herself imagine a future in which Edgar no longer existed in her life, and it was open to new possibilities.

Chapter Eight

Helen returned home just in time to boil eggs on the stove for Amy's sandwich while she changed her clothes. She would make chopped egg sandwiches and open a can of soup after she and Amy returned home.

She waited outside the kindergarten building and watched children run through the door. Amy was being a slowpoke. Finally, once most of the other children had already been picked up, Helen went inside. The room was empty. She found the teacher and asked about Amy.

"Amy?" the teacher said, her face vacant as though she were struggling to remember who Amy was.

"Yes, Amy Brooks, my daughter," Helen said, struggling to keep her voice calm.

"All the children have left," the teacher said.

"Amy has to be in here someplace. Or did she leave with another child?"

"The parent would have reported such arrangements to us." She frowned at Helen. "You would have had to call the principal to arrange that."

The righteous tone in her voice infuriated Helen. "I didn't want her to leave with anyone but me."

"She was very stubborn about staying out when I called them all in for snacks."

Helen took a deep breath. "So you just ignored her and left her unattended?

"She cried," the teacher said, biting her lips to form a pout.

Helen noticed triangles of sweat under the woman's arms. "Stupid woman," she exploded with anger. "She's only five years old and you left her alone to make her own judgment about safety. Let me talk to your supervisor."

The teacher squared her shoulders. "I'm in charge today."

"Heaven help us," Helen said, unable to be polite. It appeared to her that the personnel in this facility were incompetent. She had failed to notice this. She should have interviewed all of the employees and observed them at work before trusting them with Amy. This was her fault. But there would be enough time for self-recrimination later. For now, she needed to focus on the most pressing issue at hand: finding Amy.

She ran past the woman and inside the building to Amy's room. Four or five children were seated at desks. Amy was here. Helen knew it. "Amy," she called loudly. There was no answer. She squeezed her body into Amy's desk-chair, her legs sticking out in the aisle. She flipped up the lid to see drawings, cookie crumbs, and a tiny white sweater. A scent of honey, Amy's favorite, wafted upward. Helen's fingers felt like separate tools with which she pressed the crumbs to her lips. Their sweetness made her choke and cough nonstop. She ran out to the hall and bent over the drinking fountain where she swallowed water as though she had been parched for days.

Just one clue was all she needed. Back in the classroom, pictures of suns, raindrops, and flowers showed only what Amy liked to draw. Nothing else. Her head felt heavy. Drawings on the wall, the blackboard, a border of cardboard letters and the teacher's desk floated as though blurred by fog. She leaned on the wall to steady herself as she walked to the door. The plaster scratched her arm.

Once outside, she called: "Amy. Amy. Come to Mommy." She repeated the words in front of bushes, behind buildings, and at every tree until she began to run out of breath.

"I know you're back there. Olley, olley oxen free." They had played hide and seek so many times that Amy would know that meant she had won and it was time to come back. But she didn't come. Helen continued searching and yelling. Her words echoed in her ears: "Amy. It's time to go home."

No answer.

"Amy, stop playing games. Come here this minute."

The lack of a response hung on the air. She should not have brought Amy to Vanport. She should not have come here at all. This was her punishment for being selfish; Amy had run away. What was wrong with Helen? She hadn't noticed that Amy was unhappy.

Something under a tree, partially covered by leaves, startled her. Was it Amy? No. Amy just wandered off and would be back soon. A body. Not Amy. She poked her shaking hand into the leaves. They fluttered and spread a dank odor. It was just a pile of leaves, but she couldn't stop her pulse from beating her temples. Amy was not in the yard.

In the distance, building after building, acres of land and rows of ships, startled her. Newspaper pictures of missing children and of bones that showed up later flashed through her mind. She heard a scream and looked around before she realized the noise came from her mouth. Would Amy be inside or outside? Helen felt tears roll down her cheeks. She took a deep breath and staggered back to the kindergarten room where she opened every door and cupboard. The rolls of poster paper and boxes of crayons blurred.

She wandered up and down the long hallway, stopping at each room to check large and small desks, poke into every closet and every cupboard. Notebooks floated with the rolls of paper and boxes of crayons. She ran back down the hall to make sure she hadn't missed any rooms. Her breath came in gasps. Sweat gushed from her armpits. What could she do? She had to find Amy.

She ran outside. Lights flashed in front of the yard. After her eyes adjusted to the glare, Helen saw some cars park. Sunlight bounced off the shadow of a stranger. Voices came as though someone were talking through a tin can. Were they playing telephone the way her brother and she had done?

"Hey, guys, a woman's in shock here. Maybe we should take her to the hospital. Over here, Sheriff."

Words cluttered her ears as if she were watching a bad movie.

Everything came back to her. Amy was missing and these officials must think something terrible had happened to her.

A man in a khaki uniform with a large star-shaped badge on his shirt approached her. He looked down at the lawn. "Dang, I almost stepped in this stuff."

Helen followed his gaze, not knowing what she would find. She concentrated on his finger as it pointed to some small dog poop.

"This is the oldest trick in the book but it always works. Looks as if the kidnapper must have enticed your child with a dog."

"Kidnap? That can't be. She is playing somewhere. Look for her." Tears sizzled on her hot face. "Amy wanted a dog so badly. I should have bought her one."

"I'm Sheriff Hanlon, ma'am. I know this is difficult for you."

He smelled of toothpaste and stale deodorant. Helen stared at the black hair coming out of a mole on his cheek. If she kept looking at it, focusing on this one small detail in front of her, then maybe she wouldn't have to think about Amy in danger. It didn't work.

"This couldn't be about money," Hanlon said as his eyes scanned Helen's baggy coveralls and cumbersome shoes.

"Money?" Helen tried to think. Lots of people had more money than she did.

He called to another man, wearing a badge like his. "Hey, Bud, go inside and call the FBI, then come outside and see if you can get some footprints here."

"No way. The ground is mush from last night's rain.

"Yeah? Well, it looks like it will be pouring in a few minutes so take your best shot."

Their clipped dialogue sounded too much like the lines from a Humphrey Bogart movie. Call the FBI? Her legs folded under her. The sheriff caught her. Helen had to be strong. Though her legs felt soft as marshmallows, she pulled away from him. Her eyes were heavy. She lowered her eyelids, wrapped her finger around some hair, and twirled the strand. Clouds rolled across the sky and blotted all light while rain pounded her face. She just stood there until her hair turned into a soggy clump. Then she took a scarf from her coat pocket and covered her head. The sheriff linked his arm to hers and tried to move her toward his car.

She planted her feet on the ground and tensed her body. "I am not leaving here until I find Amy."

A dark car pulled up in front of the building. Some men wearing navy-blue jackets with badges on the lapels got out. Helen recognized Dan. His straight shoulders and swinging arms exuded confidence. If only she could share that. If only she could believe he would find Amy and make this all go away. Before this, she'd been struck by how handsome and competent he was. But now he just seemed like an ordinary person, and she needed Superman.

He looked directly at her, his face so close she could see the worry lines on his forehead.

Why was he worried? Did his experience tell him Amy was dead? Helen's questions were too scary even to contemplate. She couldn't hold the tears back anymore. They gushed down her face. "What am I doing at this shipyard? If I had stayed in California with Edgar this would never have happened."

"It's not your fault," Dan said. He pulled a handkerchief from his pocket and handed it to her.

She stared at the handkerchief. "I knew I shouldn't have been a witness. That's what this is about, isn't it?"

"Not necessarily."

Helen wanted more assurance than those words. "Necessarily. What is that supposed to mean?"

"I know you're worried and I understand." He held Helen's hand. "I will investigate every detail of this case."

With her other hand she grasped his. "Promise me you'll find Amy."

"Our agency has a superb record."

"What about the Lindbergh baby?" Helen asked, frightening herself.

The sheriff and Dan moved far enough away for her not to hear them. The only words she could make out were *violent crimes*.

She raised her voice. "Violent? What do you know about Amy that you aren't telling me?" Helen didn't even recognize her own shrill voice.

Don came over and put his arm around her shoulders. "That's just FBI jargon. We will consider all angles. Is your husband still in town?"

"I think he left yesterday," Helen said. "Maybe he didn't go back. Maybe he stayed and took Amy somewhere."

"I'll alert our San Francisco office about your husband."

The trees seemed to swirl around Helen. Nothing made sense. She wanted to stay in Dan's arms and let time go backwards. If she had met him earlier, before she ever met Edgar, her life would have been so much better. But then she wouldn't have had Amy. The thought reminded her that Amy was gone. Gone. "Amy, where are you?"

Chapter Nine

Dan was torn. Helen looked like a lost child. He felt pulled to her the way his poor fichus leaned toward the sun. He squared his shoulders, hoping the posture would make him act professionally, and called to the Evidence Recovery Crew, who had just arrived: "Okay guys, listen to me. Search every square inch inside and out. Don't overlook any scrap of paper or other possible clues, especially shoe prints, even the ones that have been compromised by other foot traffic." He realized his voice was harsh, but he needed to stay in control, professional. That was better than letting his emotions take over. If only he could stop for a minute and hug Helen or make her feel better.

The chief had paired Dan with Albert Hanson from Violent Crimes, the department that dealt with kidnapping. Dan had seen him around the Bureau and had never liked him. Albert was a compulsive worrier and was overly ambitious. Now, Dan was stuck with him. Dan knew that Albert would try and take over even though the crime happened at a defense plant, which was Dan's territory. *Look at me, acting like a kid.* Albert had more experience with kidnappers and Dan would work with him. But he wouldn't let him take over. It had happened on Dan's watch and he needed be the one to solve this.

" We're going to find Amy." As soon as the words were out, Dan knew he had broken the taboo on making such promises. He should have known better. Sometimes the professional stoic demeanor demanded by the FBI was too much. He had to get Helen off the site so he could concentrate on his investigation. "Let Sheriff Hanlon here take you home. I'll be there as soon as my team finishes."

"Hey, I've got something here," the technician said as he picked up a cigarette butt. "It's sopping wet." He showed it to Helen, asking if she recognized the brand, if any of her acquaintances smoked it.

Helen stopped. Her voice sounded as though she would break down any minute. "All my friends smoke and most of the people at the shipyard. But I never paid attention to what cigarettes they were smoking."

Dan didn't want to involve Helen, so he quickly said, "Bag it," and led her to Hanlon's car. Helen froze in front of the car door. "I can't leave. When Amy comes back, if I'm not here, she will be scared."

Dan spoke softly. "She knows me. I'll come to your apartment very soon."

"But Amy will be frightened," Helen pleaded.

"She will be fine," Dan said with more assurance than he felt.

"How can you expect me to leave without my child?" Helen wept so hard her shoulders shook.

Dan took his handkerchief from his pocket and wiped her eyes. "You can really help us by taking the sheriff to your apartment."

"Help Amy?"

He bent over Helen and held her arm as she climbed onto the running board and into the car. Before returning to the scene, he watched the sheriff drive away, the swoosh of wheels laboring to roll on the uneven ground. He returned to the yard and walked slowly around, under the swings and slides. Just ordinary. The area where the sheriff had found the dog doo was only a flowerbed. He strode down the walkway to the red brick school building. It looked so peaceful. The criminals had to leave something, some clue that they could track Amy down by. He went into the school office and used the phone to request officers from the Canine Squad. Waiting for them, he ambled down the hall, which appeared to be immaculate. In the kindergarten room, the teacher directed him to Amy's desk. The children stared at him. "Never go with strangers," a child said.

"Yes, never," another one said.

Dan looked at all the boys and girls, so small and vulnerable in their crisp cotton dresses and shorts and shirts, their eyes wide open. "You are right. Never go with strangers even if they have a dog, or promise to get you one." He took a sweater from Amy's desk. It was so small. He would rather shoot it out with criminals, catch embezzlers, or even sit on a dull surveillance. He hated kidnapping cases the most, especially the ones where small children had been taken. And this one was worse because he felt a personal involvement.

He couldn't forget the time he had given Helen a ride to pick up Amy. The little girl had skipped alongside her mother, the two of them laughing, their red hair flying. Now, Helen was riding to her home where the sheriff would probably scare the bejesus out of her with his questioning. Dan would not tell Helen the percentage of kidnapped children who were never found, or of the equal number that were found raped and beaten to death. Taboos be damned, he wouldn't let those things happen to Amy, if he had any power to stop it.

Sweater in hand, Dan took deliberate steps back to the scene, where he handed it to the Canine trainer. The dogs sniffed and slobbered over the sweater before running, nose down, along the grounds. Dan and the officers followed them from the playground to the school and ended up inside the kindergarten room.

Finally, some good news. The dogs had not dug into any dirt or lawn, which meant Amy had not been buried. The bad news was they didn't sniff at any of the closets or other possible hiding places. The dogs only stopped at normal places, which meant there was not even one lead. Albert greeted Dan. "I told Evidence to dust for prints in the victim's classroom, and I'm going to send the cigarette butt to Washington. It's a long shot. If anyone can find something, the boys at that lab will."

Dan simply nodded his head. What good would it do to tell Albert the technicians had already done that or that the cigarette butt was useless? Maybe Albert's style of overkill would get results at some point.

Whether they would or not, Dan was stuck with him.

The dogs took off again along the front walkway, onto the road, sniffed for a few feet and stopped.

"You find something?" Dan said to the handler, preparing for the worst.

"Yep," an officer answered. "The dogs stopped here. It sure as heck looks like the child has been taken by car at this point."

Dan looked at his watch. "She could be anywhere that could be reached in two hours."

Albert took over abruptly. "An autopsy of Erich Talbott gave us some important evidence. Besides the blow to his head, there were scratch marks on his arms and face. The scratches were inflicted by small but long fingernails, most probably from a woman." Albert said as he took a tablet from his pocket and flipped through some papers, scanned a page and said, "The scratches are of a defensive manner as though the woman felt a need to protect herself."

Why the hell was he talking about this now? Dan forced himself to listen, but he couldn't concentrate on anything except finding the little girl.

Albert continued, "The murder was executed by a woman. If it was done in self-defense, then we have yet to find the motive for this abduction."

Exhaustion rolled over Dan. He needed to check on Helen, needed to tear himself away from this contest with Albert. Yet, this *super agent* needed to be stopped. "You've been assuming that the kidnapper was desperate to stop Mrs. Brooks from testifying." He paused. "There has to be more. If the killer was defending herself, it doesn't follow that she would commit another crime, such as kidnapping."

"Not necessarily," Albert said as if he were lecturing Dan. "The killer could be Mrs. Yamamoto."

As usual, Albert had to have the last word. For a change, Dan decided not to let him do this. "There are other suspects we should consider before jumping to conclusions." Dan saw Albert's eye twitch, a sure sign that he was upset. Good, Dan had gotten to him, had let him see what it was like to be outdone.

After Albert left, Dan could only stand and look at the road. It seemed to stretch for miles. No cars, no human beings on this road that appeared to be endless. The emptiness reminded Dan of the hopelessness in finding this child. What difference did it make whether he or Albert won the competition?

Chapter Ten

As the sheriff followed Helen into her apartment, she could feel the walls move closer and closer. They would smother her. Not even a kitchen, just a counter, and the living room barely had space for anyone to sit. She and Hanlon sat in two stiff chairs facing each other. They could play musical chairs but there was no space and Amy wasn't there. Amy would have been better off in her own room in their spacious house in Atherton. This entire apartment would have fit into their master bathroom.

Sheriff Hanlon interrupted her thoughts. "The agent will need something that your daughter wore recently."

"Wore recently?"

"A T-shirt or pajamas."

Trying not to think about why they needed this garment, Helen walked into the bedroom she and Amy shared, and walked along the wall, tracing each cloud, each sun, and all the trees in the pictures that Amy had drawn. She grabbed a nightgown from Amy's dresser and noticed a box in the drawer. Helen took off the lid to see rubber bands that looked like tiny worms. Amy had been saving this for the school's rubber drive. Helen hoped she could remember to put some more rubber bands in there.

She stopped next to Amy's bed. The quilt was bunched up as though Amy were asleep beneath it.

Amy, wake up. Mommy is here. Wake up.

Helen reached out and touched the cover. Nothing but fluff. She ran past the bed and out of the room.

The sheriff stood up. Helen stared at him. He was a stranger. She didn't remember walking the short distance into the living room.

"I'll take that now," he said

She sat on the stiff chair, clasped the cotton in her fingers, and rubbed it on her face. No one was going to take any more of Amy away. But the more rational part of her knew that he was trying to help, so reluctantly she handed it over.

"I'm sorry. He will want a picture of the child, too."

The sheriff's face faded as she resisted this, too. "Amy?"

"Yes, a picture. It will help us find her."

Helen thought his face looked like Donald Duck when he spoke. She walked the few feet to the kitchen counter and retrieved the wallet from her purse. When she tried to remove the photo of Amy from behind the clear plastic display, she bent over the drain board and sobbed. Water gushed like an ocean and Helen floated and floated, swimming to find Amy.

Finally, she sponged her face with cold water and dried it with a hand-towel.

Footsteps startled her. She turned around to see Dan. He dwarfed the miniscule kitchen. Before she knew what she was doing, she ran into his arms and rested her head on his shoulder, drinking in the smell of his aftershave lotion, the slick feel of his jacket. For a second she believed that Dan could make this nightmare go away. Together they returned and sat on the living room sofa.

Dan took the picture and nightgown from Helen. "The technician should be here soon," he informed her, just as the doorbell chimed. "That's probably him." He got up to open the door, and from the distance she heard two male voices that came across so soft she couldn't make out what they said. Why was he answering the door in her house? She walked to the front door. Dan had let a man inside. "Tim here will set up a phone tap and be in your living room all night."

Helen looked at the kid. He still had fuzz on his chin and his Adam's apple sat on his throat like a ping-pong ball. "Why is he here?"

"This is protocol. He will set up a phone tap. You might get a phone call from Amy's kidnapper, or someone might try and harm you. Either way, this will let us trace the calls to find out where she might be."

"Why did they take my baby?" Helen felt the sofa cushion beneath her but didn't remember sitting down.

Dan sat next to Helen on the sofa and looked at her. "We don't know, but that is what we are going to find out. Earlier, you told me about your husband wanting custody of your daughter."

Helen nodded. "But he wouldn't do this. He behaved badly with everyone else, but he adored Amy and wouldn't upset her by taking her away so suddenly. He didn't mind betraying me with other women, but he is always sweet with Amy. That is why I put up with his shenanigans for so many years." Tears rolled down her face. "Knowing Edgar, I could..." Helen couldn't remember what she was going to say.

"We'll find her," Dan promised.

Helen saw his mouth move but didn't hear any words. "You've got to find the real kidnapper." Helen sunk farther and farther into the sofa. She would disappear. Disappear. She floated away to the shipyard, face after face of strangers. Which one took Amy?

Chapter Eleven

Amy woke up in a strange bed in a room much smaller than the room where she and Mommy slept. The walls were dirty and the room smelled like cooked cabbage. She ran to the door but it was locked. This was her fault. She shouldn't have followed the man with the dog. It was the same kind she had seen in the window at the pet store. It was small and tan with floppy ears. Her mother had said the dog was a Cocker Spaniel. The man who walked the dog had told her she could play with it. She remembered skipping along beside him. He put a rag on her face.

That was the last thing she remembered. Now she was in this ugly room. How long did she sleep? Maybe she died and came back. Amy started to cry.

The woman, who had told Amy to call her Diane, came into the room. She had thick lips and smelled like dead flowers. "You shut your damn mouth."

Amy had never heard a woman swear and it scared her. "I want my mommy."

"Well, you can't have her."

The lady grabbed her hand so tight it hurt really bad and dragged her down the dark hall. She wouldn't even let Amy go pee. The lady's lips got bigger. Ugly, ugly, ugly. Amy started crying again. The woman slapped her face. It burned. They came into the kitchen. A man who looked like the one who washed their windows in California was talking into a telephone. He stopped when the lady and Amy came in.

Diane shoved Amy toward the man. His breath smelled like onions. He put the phone against her ear. "Talk to your mom."

"I want to come home, Mommy!"

The man took the phone away.

Diane put her arm around Amy. "Okay, I've done that. Now can I have the girl?"

"Not so fast," the man said.

"You promised."

"If there's trouble, we'll have to get rid of her."

"How?"

"You don't need to know."

The lady hugged Amy. "You aren't going to hurt her. I won't let you."

The man yanked the lady's arm and reached for her throat. Amy was more scared than when she rode her bike for the first time, or when her mommy and daddy argued. She was so scared she wet her pants. She was a bad girl. Mommy told her never to go with strangers. But this man had a puppy and he said she could have it. The lady took her back to the room. When she left, Amy sucked her thumb. Mommy had told her not to do that but she would know why Amy had to. She choked to quiet her crying.

Chapter Twelve

Once Dan and the sheriff had left, Helen brushed her teeth, fell into bed, and cried. The phone rang. She looked at her clock. Nine o'clock. She must have fallen asleep. She threw on her chenille robe and ran towards the kitchen. A stranger jumped up from the sofa and followed her.

"What are you doing here?" Helen asked.

"I'm the phone technician," he said as he bent over the phone equipment on the drain board and waved his arm to motion her to answer.

"Technician?"

"Please answer the phone," he said before handing her the receiver.

Helen remembered. The receiver shook in her hand as she answered weakly.

"We have your daughter." The voice was garbled but Helen heard the message.

She fell into the straight-backed chair. "Let me talk to her."

"Not so fast."

"You should return her before you get in trouble."

"Hey, lady, I'm making the calls here. When you have the money?"

The room blurred into gray specks. She cleared her throat to steady her voice. "How do I know you have her?"

There was a pause.

"I want to come home, Mommy." She heard Amy's voice through the receiver.

"Soon, Sweetie," Helen managed to say. "Are you all right?"

The strange voice came back on. Helen strained to hear him over the patter of water from the leaking sink faucet. "It will cost you fifty thousand bucks to get your kid back."

Helen tried to recognize the voice but it sounded fuzzy. "It will take me some time to get the money," she said.

"I'll call you tomorrow night and tell you where to drop off the money. No police." There was a pause. "You get rid of all the law that is in your place and you come alone or we'll kill her."

Kill? Helen had to be strong. "I don't have any police here." The metallic smell of boiled eggs overpowered her.

"Hey, lady, I weren't born yesterday."

The tiny kitchen closed in on her. The chair seat pressed against her skin as she listened to the dial tone's tap, tap, until the technician took the receiver from her and placed it in the cradle.

"Will I ever see my baby?" Helen said, willing him to say she would.

The man pointed at his equipment. "I'll get a trace from the call."

Why was that ugly thing on her drain board? Helen knew the technician was just saying that to make her feel better. She would never see Amy again. She ran into the bedroom and buried her head under the pillow so she wouldn't have to look at Amy's empty bed.

Helen felt as though someone had pulled the ground out from under her and she was floating on the mattress. How was she going to find the money for the kidnapper? She had $20,000 in her savings account, but she needed that to fight for custody in case Edgar sued her again. If she had to use it for ransom, she would. From the monthly salary saving bond deductions, she had $2,000.00. If the house would sell, she would get half, which would be around $14,000.00. Even if the house did sell, she still wouldn't have enough. But if she bargained with the kidnapper, he might hurt Amy.

The realtor in Atherton had given Helen her number. She rifled through her purse, fished it out from the bottom and dialed Florence Hardy's number. Florence answered on the first ring. "I read about your daughter in the *Chronicle*. I'm so sorry. I hope you find her soon."

"That's what I'm calling about. I need the money to get her back." Helen regretted giving out that information. "Any bites on our house?"

"There's been lots of interest but it's so difficult to find a time to show that is convenient for your ex-husband."

A red haze spread across the room as though the fire inside Helen had exploded. Finally, she said, "Don't you have a key?"

"He preferred not to give us one." Florence sounded whiney.

Rage pounded every inch of Helen's body and there was no place to release it. Edgar didn't want to sell the house. She couldn't deal with that now. "I'll call my lawyer tomorrow morning."

Given the wartime speed limit of thirty-five miles an hour, Helen wouldn't be able to race down Sandy Boulevard like she had done before, so it would take half an hour to get to her mother's house. She decided to go immediately, and if her mother were out she would just sit and wait for her. She had told her mother what had happened to Amy over the shipyard office phone, trying to sound less scared than she was. She didn't want her mother to say, "I told you so," or blame her for having put Amy in a dangerous new living situation. But now she needed comfort and didn't know where else to turn.

When Helen drove her car onto the approach to the bridge, the span was open and several cars were stopped in front of her. If she could only think straight, she would have called her mother to make sure she was home.

While she waited, Helen decided it was time for her to try and find Amy on her own. Maybe Dan knew something about Charlotte that he was not telling, facts too frightening for Helen to hear. Charlotte could have found out about Helen being a witness, about her reporting to the authorities that Helen had seen a woman with her ballerina walk on the deck of the ship. But then she wouldn't call for money, unless that was to mislead everyone. No. Charlotte was too nice to kidnap a child.

The cars started up and Helen repeated the words, "What does Dan know?" to the rhythm of her tires rolling on the uneven pavement, bump by bump, until she pulled up in front of her parents' house.

Lights shone through the living room windows. What if her mother had company?

Helen rushed up the steps and rang the bell. Heat hung in the air but Helen shivered. When her mother opened the door, her expression changed from the raised eyebrows of surprise to a sympathetic smile. "I'm so glad you came," she said as she led Helen into the living room "Can you spend the night?"

"I wish I could but I need to be home in case someone calls," Helen said as she followed her mother into the kitchen, where she fixed Helen a whiskey sour. She emptied some crackers from a box of Cheeze-Its into a crystal bowl. "Have you had dinner?"

"I'm not hungry."

"You must keep up your strength." Her mother surveyed Helen's face and frowned. "I made a tuna casserole for dinner and I'll slice some tomatoes from our garden."

Helen followed her into the kitchen and watched her mother pull the food out of the icebox. She remembered gathering around the ice truck with all the neighborhood kids so they could watch the man carry the large chunk up the back steps. Then they would grab chips of ice and suck them. Helen had deprived Amy of a normal neighborhood. If Amy—not *if*, no, never say *if*—when Amy came back, they would move to a house. Helen gulped her drink and waited until the bourbon flowed into her body and gave her the courage to approach her mother to voice the request she had come to make.

"The kidnappers want fifty thousand dollars," she said at last.

"Goodness, that's a lot," her mother said.

Helen took a deep breath and exhaled. Under any normal circumstances, she would rather dance naked at a nightclub than ask her mother for money. But this was for Amy. "I have thirty-two thousand dollars and I need to borrow eighteen thousand," she managed.

"Oh, Honey, you know I would help you if I could," her mother said, "but we used all of our savings and borrowed money on this house to pay the cost of bringing Aaron over here."

Helen twirled a strand of hair around her finger to calm herself and remembered Uncle Aaron, a short man with a wart on his cheek. He used to play magic tricks with her. Though his sleight of hand was so obvious, Helen had played along with him. She knew she was being unreasonable, but at that moment she resented the money going to her uncle instead of to get Amy back. Helen forced herself to ask about her father.

"It doesn't look good. He defended President Roosevelt when a large number of people called him an anti-Semite for sending a boat full of Jews back to Germany when their boat was near Miami. But now that your dad needs the president's help in bringing Aaron out of Sweden, the president refuses to help."

"Sweden?"

"Aaron helps Jews escape from Germany. Recently he found out he's in danger in Sweden also."

"Dad will find a way. That's Washington," Helen tried to sound positive. "The president has to appear one way with the State Department and he can still help Dad quietly."

Her mother smiled, slightly. "I hope you're right." She paused. "Honey, why don't you ask Edgar for the money?"

Helen hesitated. She knew that her mother liked Edgar but she had to answer. "I'm afraid he'll demand custody of Amy if he gives me the money," she said.

"That's ridiculous. You're entitled to half of the house in Atherton."

"It hasn't sold yet."

Her mother's face turned crimson. "Nonsense. He just hasn't tried. You promise him the world but get the money. Deal with him later."

Maybe Helen had misjudged her mother. "Yes, that's what I will do."

Helen had been so involved in the conversation that she hadn't noticed her mother had heated the casserole and sliced some tomatoes. They carried the food into the breakfast room.

"You won't be able to save this for another meal. Will your ration stamps last until the end of the month?

"With your father away, I've got plenty of stamps," her mother said.

Helen had thought that she would never eat again, but steam from the casserole carried a tangy scent of onion and fish that reminded her she hadn't eaten all day.

When they finished eating, her mother served tea and cookies. Helen took a few sips of tea. "I better get back if I'm going to call Edgar."

"Let me know if he refuses. I'll try and sell some of my jewelry."

Chapter Thirteen

Helen walked into her apartment and almost tripped over the pile of papers that Amy had been saving for the school paper drive. Helen would have to take them to the school. No, she was going to wait for Amy to do it.

She placed another paper on the pile before she called the hotel and asked for Edgar's room. The woman told her he had checked out that morning.

"Are you sure? Maybe you should ring him to make certain."

"Someone else has already checked into the room he vacated."

"Exactly what time did he leave?"

"I have no idea. Checkout time is noon."

Helen hung up without saying anything more. What was she going to do? Even if Edgar had left early in the morning, he would most likely stay over night in Redding or another small town.

When she got into bed, her legs tensed as though they wanted to keep walking on their own. What if the crooks wanted their money before she could reach Edgar? She felt as though a jumping jack had been planted in her chest.

The technicians coming in and out of her apartment drove her crazy, and waiting for the phone call was unbearable. She went into the kitchen and poured some sherry into a glass. The sweet liquid slid down her throat but didn't dull the jiggles in her body. *Amy, Amy, where are you?* She took several gulps straight from the bottle.

After sleeping for a short time, she sat up in bed. She felt as though a vise were clamped on either side of her forehead. What was she thinking about when she drank all that sherry? She needed to think straight now and not have a hangover. She never drank that much, and now she needed to be alert. Edgar could have taken Amy to make Helen look bad. But he wouldn't upset Amy like that—or would he? If someone wanted to scare Helen out of identifying the killer, they would have said so instead of asking for money.

She looked at her watch on the bedside table. It was 5:30. Edgar was probably sleeping somewhere. The aroma of coffee wafted into her room. She put on her chenille robe and followed the scent to the kitchen, where the technician was inhaling the steam from his coffee cup. Given the rate at which he made pots of coffee, Helen worried if she would run out of ration stamps. She was only allowed one pound of coffee to last five weeks.

"Want some?" Tim said as he reached for another cup from the crowded shelf in the only cupboard.

"I might as well. There's no point in trying to sleep." Helen took a sip of the coffee he had poured for her. This man seemed too young to be efficient. What could she do? He was her only chance to find Amy.

"What kind of signals did you get from the kidnapper's call last night?" she asked at last.

"Our equipment isn't as efficient as I would like. It was used mainly for tapping phones and listening to conversations. Work was done recently to identify locations, but it isn't exact." He paused. "Sorry to say, but they've got a long way to go. I would say that it's on the East side, possibly Northeast. I picked up a range between 32nd and 41st."

Helen sipped her coffee and thought about her parents' house. She felt as limp as a popped balloon. "That area has some fine neighborhoods, streets where criminals would stick out," she offered hopefully, trying to help.

"There are pockets of run-down areas. I've tuned up my equipment and hope to get more signals when they call back about where to drop the money."

At first Helen thought his answer was discouraging, but it was all she had. She needed money. The money would get Amy back. Edgar had the money. She dialed their California phone number and listened to twelve rings before hanging up. Where was he? He ran away with Amy. Helen just knew he did. No money. She decided to give Dan one more chance and then she was going to find Amy on her own. She waited another half hour until seven o'clock to call him.

When she heard Dan's voice through the wire, she wanted to hang up. No. Amy needed her.

"Hello," he repeated, with annoyance.

"They called." Helen tried to arrange the words but she just blurted whatever she could. "Money. It's hopeless. I can't get the money. I'm going to find her on my own."

"I'll be there right away. Wait for me."

When the doorbell rang, Helen was afraid. Either a stranger at her door, or Dan had used a siren to get there this fast.

Edgar's voice came through the door. "Helen, it's me. Let me in."

She had to force her fingers around the doorknob to open the door. "Where have you been?" she asked before she opened the screen door. "I've been trying to get you. Do you have Amy?"

Edgar walked into the living room. "Absolutely not. I read the story in the paper. How could you lose our daughter?"

"I didn't lose her. You took her."

"Wrong again."

"I called the hotel. They said you had checked out."

"I told them I didn't want to be disturbed," Edgar said, obviously pleased with his action.

"Why?"

"I needed to plan how to find Amy." Edgar surveyed the apartment. "You seem surprised to see me." He walked inside and sat on the sofa. "You expect me to stay away when you have messed up everything?" Edgar paused, probably to emphasize his derision, and waved his arm to encompass the apartment. "I can't believe you brought our daughter to live in a hole like this and didn't watch her closely enough."

Helen avoided sitting next to him and slid into the chair, which was still too close. She struck back. "Are you sure you didn't take Amy?"

"Really, Helen, don't be so ridiculous."

"Someone has her and we haven't rejected the idea that you could have hired a criminal."

"We?" Edgar asked, mockingly. "So now you are cozy with the investigators?"

Helen looked straight at him. "You're pathetic." What did she ever see in him? He looked like a store mannequin, stiff as his starched shirt.

He wasn't silent for long. "I understand you are under a strain and I will ignore your rudeness."

Helen had no intention of sparring with Edgar. "Someone called me, and wants fifty thousand dollars and will call tomorrow." Helen felt like a bag lady, begging for money. With her shoes flat on the rug, she pushed her chair away from Edgar, almost to the kitchen. "Did you put the criminal up to it?"

Edgar studied his shiny manicured nails. "Just to show you how forgiving I am, I'll call my bank tomorrow and get the money."

"Right away. Can you get it right away?"

"Of course, that means I will get custody of Amy."

Helen felt alive for the first time since Amy was taken. This was just what she had feared, as she had voiced that fear to her mother. "I don't understand why you want custody so badly. You work all day."

Edgar tilted his head into a superior pose. "You left and took her away from me. No one gets away with treating me like that."

"You jerk. You're using this horrible thing to take advantage of me, and treating Amy like a possession. All I want is for Amy to be safe again. And if you even try to get custody I will report you to the FBI for selling on the black market. Yes, I know you were bringing in tires to sell without ration stamps."

"You're a lunatic."

"And I know what else you were doing there."

He sat forward on the sofa. "I don't want to hear any more from you."

The doorbell rang.

Helen was glad to be interrupted. She could have brought up his lying about his asthma to get out of serving in the war, but decided to keep that as a hidden resource.

"It's about time," she said to Dan as she opened the door. "Oops, I'm sorry. You are not the one provoking me."

Dan smiled and walked over to speak with the technician.

Edgar stepped between them. "I'm Edgar, her husband."

Dan extended his arm. They shook hands.

"When did you get here?" Dan said.

"I came up two days ago to visit my in-laws. I would have returned home, if this horrible event hadn't happened to Amy."

Helen studied Dan's face to see if he believed that nonsense. His polite interest didn't change. He was so darn good at that.

"So you're the big-shot FBI," Edgar continued. "Why aren't you out there looking for our daughter?"

"We are. Which reminds me, you sued for custody of your daughter, didn't you?"

Edgar twisted his face into a smart-aleck pose that Helen abhorred. "You bet I did, and there is probably one sorry judge for not awarding it to me."

Dan laughed, sounding overly jolly. "You're right there. It must be frustrating for you, knowing you could do a better job." He paused. "When is the last time you saw your daughter?"

"You son of a bitch, why aren't you out looking for Amy as we speak?"

Dan sat on the other chair, took a deep breath and exhaled. "Sorry, but I would be in big trouble with my boss if I overlooked anyone who had contact with the mother or child."

"If you think this is going to get you any closer to Helen, I should tell you she got a quickie divorce and I intend to poke holes in it and bring Helen and our daughter back home after this is over."

"Shut up, Edgar," Helen said. She had never talked to him like this before. It made her feel better than she had for days. *Shut up. Shut up.* Helen couldn't wait for the next opportunity to repeat the words.

"I better get back to my hotel," Edgar said as he walked to the door.

Helen walked with him. "I'll keep you posted."

Edgar's eyes shifted through the opening to the bedroom, to the small square of a kitchen, and settled on the living area. "You gave up all you had for this?"

"You sound like a broken record," Helen said.

Edgar ignored her statement. "Don't bother informing me about Amy. I'm going to get involved, too."

"You stay out of it. The police and the FBI are working on it and you will just get in the way."

"I know more important people than you ever will." Edgar slammed the door as he left.

Helen stood by the door and turned slowly to observe the apartment. She had been stupid to think that she and Amy could make a home in this miniscule space, survive, let alone flourish among the shipyard workers. She sat next to Dan, who had moved to the sofa. "I'm sorry you had to hear all that."

Dan grinned. "I've come upon worse."

"They're going to call me tomorrow to tell me where to leave the money."

"Great. The agents and I will be right behind you."

Helen stood up. "You can't have your men there. The kidnapper will kill Amy if I don't do what he told me to."

Dan followed Helen and put his arm around her shoulders. "Her only chance is for us to find her. We're experienced in disguise. He'll never know we're there."

Helen shrugged off his arm. "No, you don't mean that. Say you don't. He'll return her when I give him the money."

"I do mean it," Dan said. "We will find him and rescue Amy."

"He won't return her even if I do what he says?"

Dan moved closer to her. "No one knows. It's imperative that we are present."

Helen started crying. Dan pulled her to him. "Let's sit down."

She pulled away. "I don't believe you. You are too influenced by your position with the FBI. I'll hold you responsible for my daughter's safety if this fails." Helen couldn't say the word: die.

Chapter Fourteen

Helen's head felt as though popcorn were popping inside. While she knew that Dan was experienced doing this work, she couldn't stand the idea that he would endanger Amy in any way. She had to take action. The only thing she could think of was to snoop around the shipyard. After Dan left, she checked her ration book for gas stamps and decided not to drive, though it was only three miles to the shipyard.

The few latecomers on the bus greeted her but didn't sit in the seat next to her, probably because they didn't know what to say about Amy. She understood their unease, having experienced the same discomfort when one of her parents' friends had died and she had seen the widow or widower and not known what to say. But Amy was not dead, she reminded herself, and she should not make such a comparison. She began to study the other riders but the fumes from the motor made her lightheaded and dulled her concentration. She was going to do a better job of questioning everyone than she had when Dan had ruined her visit.

The rain had stopped but the clouds were a thick deep gray. Helen's feet swished the large puddles of water on the ground. As she tried to avoid them, she felt like she was playing a game of hopscotch. If only she were welding a ship; if only Amy were playing in the schoolyard. Her eyes watered. Buildings, machinery, and war ships that had once seemed like magic, casting a spell that had excited her, now mocked her former enthusiasm and devotion.

The Administration building loomed to her left. She wanted to turn and run back to her car. What was she doing here? She didn't know if she was looking for a killer or a kidnapper or for one person who had committed both crimes.

Inside she went straight to Roxanne's desk. The chair was empty. She sat down and waited for what seemed like hours and was surprised when her watch showed that only ten minutes had passed. Carefully, she opened the deep drawer, and then glanced around to make sure no one had seen her. The hall was still empty. She pulled the drawer out farther and read the labels: Dictation, Correspondence, Schedules, and Personal. Her hand was still in the drawer, trying to slip into a folder, when she heard a click of a door-latch. Helen managed to move her hand on top of the desk and slide the drawer quietly closed. She stood up and glanced back to see who had walked out of the room. It was a woman, probably in her forties, dressed in a linen dress and white pumps with platform soles. This was not Helen's choice of style but she could appreciate that this woman probably had an important position in administration.

The woman smiled. "Can I help you?" she asked.

Helen hoped the administrator hadn't noticed her snooping. "I was looking for a piece of paper to leave Roxanne a note."

"She had a doctor's appointment. She'll be back in an hour."

Helen thanked her and tried to walk normally, though her knees were wobbly and she wanted to run. At least she knew that Roxanne had access to a lot of information, but what was in the file marked PERSONAL?

The phone was ringing when Helen returned home. She ran to see the technician. When he nodded, she picked up the phone.

"You got the money yet?" the same gruff voice demanded.

"I'll have it tomorrow afternoon," she lied. Actually, it was not exactly a lie, because she would get the money somehow.

"Five o'clock. You come alone. Get rid of the cops."

"I have."

"Listen, lady, like I told you the last time we spoke, I weren't born yesterday. You got cops coming and going. You want to see your daughter alive, you come alone."

"I will. I need to hear my daughter's voice."

"And I need to see the money."

"How do I know if she is all right?" Helen had just expressed her thoughts that Amy could be dead. She shivered.

"Take my word for it. You sure you're gonna have the money tomorrow?"

"Yes." Helen hoped her steady voice concealed her lie.

"This is what you do. Bring fifty thousand bucks in hundred dollar bills to the Greyhound bus depot and dump the dough in locker number 12. You come alone. I see any cops and the kid will be dead."

The word "dead" spun in Helen's head. She strained to form words. Finally, she said, "I'll do what you say."

The dial tone pierced her ear but she couldn't hang up. The technician, Tim, took the receiver from her hand and placed in on the cradle.

Take his word for it? That was the last thing Helen could do. She would go to the depot. Maybe she could see Amy. She needed to see her. Where was the money? She didn't stand a chance without paying the crook. She finally got the courage to speak to the technician. "Did you get a location?"

"It came from Northeast between 32nd and 41st Street. That's the best I can do."

"That is the same location as the other call. Amy is there, in that area. Why can't you find her?"

"I'm sure the agents will use this information," he said coolly.

"Money. It's all about the money. Right now I need the money to get my child back." She hated to call Dan at home, but he had to help her. By the time he answered she was crying. She swallowed her tears and told him about the phone call and her lack of money.

"Sit tight. I'll bring the money but you'll have to pay the FBI back."

"I will. I will," she said, though she didn't know how she would do that. Edgar could have given her the cash. Where was he? Anger pumped heat through her body, flushing her face.

Dan's voice caught her attention. "I'll have to go down to head-quarters and it will take me some time to record the serial numbers."

"Record? You think they'll have time to spend the money before you catch them?" Helen asked, stressing the words "catch them," them including Amy, alive and unharmed.

"It's standard procedure," Dan answered. "I'll be at your place in an hour."

Helen felt as though she were on one end of a see-saw and the person on the other end had jumped off.

Every thing she could do about the money for the kidnapper seemed to be out of her reach. Dan's description of how he had to handle the money sounded like something that would take longer than a single afternoon. She had no time to be subtle. "I need it by tomorrow," she insisted.

"I know that. Don't worry," Dan said.

"Don't worry?" she echoed, incredulous. She couldn't do anything but worry. Amy was with a criminal and she didn't have the money to get her back.

Chapter Fifteen

Dan knew that he could easily fall for Helen but it wouldn't be professional. What did he mean *could*? He had thought about nothing else since he had seen her. The image of mother and daughter walking to their apartment building, when he had waited in his car to make sure they were okay, had thrilled him. Now that memory just made him sad.

He looked around at his apartment that used to be a bedroom in this old house before the influx of shipyard workers caused a housing shortage. The high ceilings and moldings and cornices deserved more than his bland furniture: painted desk, brown sofa, and one matching chair. It needed a woman's touch. But the last woman in his life had left him wary of just that.

He thought about Rita, his ex-wife. With her blond hair and huge blue eyes and her tight dresses that caressed her curves in the right places, she was knock-down gorgeous, no question, but now that he had seen Helen, Rita seemed cheap by comparison. She never stopped complaining. He was away on assignments too much and she was lonely. They never went to nightclubs anymore. His gun made her nervous.

They were already married when she began hitting him. His self-control was constantly tested. He remembered her dancing around him and punching him in the stomach and on the face. It was like a game for her, a game designed to provoke him, to see how far she could push him, what she could make him do if she hurt him badly enough. He never hit back, but he knew how to disable her and was gentle when he stopped the attacks. Maybe she would've liked it better if he did hit her back. After their divorce, he requested an assignment in the West, as far as he could get from Washington, D.C.

If only he could get over his failed marriage enough to move on a happier future, in which he would have already met someone like Helen, just like Helen, only her child not missing.

Helen in distress had a temper. Dan marveled that Helen could be demanding when he was doing her a favor. He realized that her anxiety about Amy drove her to drop all cordiality, an understandable reaction. He had called some agents to meet him at Headquarters. It was not easy at that hour and he promised to reciprocate for each one. He needed the help and reluctantly had asked Albert.

But before he faced him, Dan sat on his upholstered chair and read the cartoons in *Esquire Magazine* about Army and Navy situations. They gave some humor to the horrendous war. Though he didn't like his FBI duties at the shipyard, the position answered his need to participate in defeating the country's enemies. He drove to the Bureau.

Now that he had his laugh, he felt more able to face the men. They had divvied up the hundred dollar bills and passed out notepads where they would copy the serial numbers. Dan noticed that while Albert performed this work with a flourish designed to show off his productivity, he kept inadvertently mixing his unrecorded bills with the marked ones. Bruce and Karl managed to get their bills in the correct piles the first time. Dan thought of a lot of remarks he could use to embarrass Albert but he had a deadline to meet.

Albert's voice broke the soft sound of shuffled paper. "Dan, are you sure you're going to be able to stay objective, here?"

"What do you mean?" Dan said, though he knew he was opening a can of worms.

Albert chuckled. "C'mon, you can't expect us to believe you aren't partial to the mother."

The two men sitting across from Dan leaned forward. Their tobacco breath flowed across the oak table.

"I'm just saying, you're vouching for this woman. Have you thought about the trouble you could be in with the Bureau if the mother can't repay the ransom?"

Dan started to tell Albert to mind his own business, but his tongue stuck on his teeth, which was a sign that he was going to stutter. After all these years, Albert had brought back Dan's weakness, like the boys in his primary school class, who had made fun of him.

As he fumed in silence and stuffed his money into the briefcase, he figured out why he was such a jerk with Albert. The man reminded him of the popular kids at school. It was Albert's self-confidence and disdain for Dan that made him relive his self-doubts. The kids had made fun of his clothes and after he answered a question in class, they imitated his stutter. They also mocked his home life.

He was the only student in his class who lived with his mother and no father. Dan wanted to go to the grammar school near their apartment, but his mother said a good education was his only chance to be a successful adult. She had worked for the school superintendent, cleaning his house, and arranged for Dan to be transferred to the better school.

He remembered waking up one morning and finding out that his father was gone. For days, he waited at the window, looking for his daddy. His mother had to carry him to the car, take him to school and along with her when she cleaned other people's houses.

When she said his father was not coming back, Dan kicked her leg. He could still remember the purple bruise spreading in the shape of a dragon up her shin.

He missed his mother and was happy that she had lived long enough to see him graduate from the University of Oregon and Willamette Law School. Of course he attended on scholarship. If his mother were looking down on him at that moment, Dan knew what she would have said. *Stand up for yourself.*

Before leaving, Dan squared his shoulders, approached Albert and said in a calm voice, "If you have no compassion for the victims or their families, maybe you ought to transfer to a different division." He strode out of the room.

Standing on Helen's front porch, Dan rang the bell. Helen opened the door. Her eyes scanned his dark suit, starched shirt, and dark tie. He had tried to make himself look exactly like Edgar, or at least close enough that if anyone was watching the house, they would mistake him for her ex-husband. Dan stepped inside and quickly walked out of sight of the windows. He held up the bulging briefcase. "Here is your fifty thousand. We recorded the serial numbers from all the bills. You better put this in a bag."

"I'm afraid the crooks will catch on if they're watching this building," Helen said, her eyes imploring him as though she needed reassurance.

Unable to promise any results, Dan tried to lighten the conversation. "Don't you think I look like your husband?"

"Don't remind me of him. I found out he isn't even trying to sell the house. And he isn't answering the phone."

"I thought he was in Portland," Dan said, trying to hide his concern.

"He checked out of the hotel yesterday morning."

"He's probably still on the road." Dan took off his tie and jacket. He wanted to move on. Helen's meeting with the kidnapper worried him. Besides, anything else he could say about Edgar might reveal how little Dan trusted him. He didn't want Helen to know, in case she suspected that his reasons for disliking her ex were not just professional but also personal. "Now, you know what you should do tomorrow?"

"I guess."

"Once this person takes the money, you take Amy, get in your car, and leave."

"What if he doesn't have Amy?" Helen asked.

"You still leave. We'll follow close in on the guy."

"You're not even supposed to be there. He said no police."

"They all say that. He won't know we're there."

"This is just another job for you." Helen sobbed. "It's my child and you don't care."

He put his arm around her. She pulled away and threw herself on the sofa. Like many other victims, she was being irrational and he wanted to comfort her. But he couldn't promise her everything would be fine when he knew the odds of her child being alive were slim. No matter how much he liked her, no matter how badly he wanted to recover her little girl, he couldn't lie to her and offer her false hope.

Chapter Sixteen

Although it was cold and dark out by the middle of the afternoon, to Helen it felt like the longest day of the year. She pulled out the picture of Rosie the Riveter and imagined inhaling her strength. Doubts flooded Helen's mind. If she hadn't come to work at the shipyard, Amy would not have been kidnapped. This was all her fault. Rosie's confident pose calmed Helen. Blaming herself accomplished nothing. She must find Amy and bring her home.

In the bedroom she forced herself to make Amy's bed and fluff up the pillows. The strawberry scent of her daughter's jawbreakers filled the air. She lay down on the bed and cried.

Helen felt as limp as the quilt under her. She missed Amy so much. Would she ever see her again? *Stop feeling sorry for yourself,* Helen thought. Her self-pity, deserved though it may have been, was doing nothing to restore her daughter to her. *I will bring Amy home.* She went to the kitchen, where she poured Rice Krispies, melted butter, and marshmallows into a baking dish and shaped it into a mold to be cut into squares. This was Amy's favorite cookie and it would be waiting for her. Helen tried to prepare for disappointment but she couldn't stop running around the apartment arranging Amy's toys and clothes.

Finally, it was four o'clock and she decided to allow herself an hour in case there was traffic or a bridge was drawn up. She put the money the FBI had given her, into an old duffle bag and drove to the bus depot on Fifth and Taylor, where she would follow the kidnapper's instructions to leave the money.

In her rearview mirror, she noticed a green Ford pull in one car back, probably not noticeable to anyone but herself. A man and a woman sat in the front seats but they didn't fool her. She knew that the FBI had some women they used as decoys.

Stopped at the intersection, Helen spotted a white Dodge turning left from Alder onto Broadway where the driver parked in front of the Broadway theatre. His car seemed inconsequential compared to the theatre's marquee and the huge fan-shaped billboard. After the signal changed, Helen noticed the Dodge pull into the line of traffic. She felt as though her heart had moved up to her throat. What if the kidnapper noticed them near the depot? Helen imagined Rosie the Riveter seated next to her and pledged not to let the FBI ruin the exchange.

Helen parked a block away from the depot, walked quickly to the front steps and rushed inside. It was almost time for the hand-off. There was no time to search for the two cars and nothing she could do about the FBI now. She had to hope they would keep a low profile, that the man who claimed not to have been born yesterday wasn't as observant as he said.

She stood in front of the tin cabinet and reached for the handle. Her arm stopped in midair. Was she an idiot? The man wanted her to leave the money and disappear without seeing Amy. Well, she hadn't been born yesterday either. Once he had the money, what was going to motivate him to hand over her daughter? Instead of leaving the ransom as he'd requested, she hugged the huge bag against her body, waited by the locker, watched the swirl of cotton skirts and listened to the clicking of brogues and sandals. She scanned children holding their mother or father's hands and did not see Amy. The smell of sour apples and tobacco made Helen gag. All these children were there and not one of them even resembled Amy. Sweat glued her blouse and skirt to her skin.

Maybe the kidnapper had seen her and wouldn't come for the money until she had deposited it and left. At that point she was willing to try anything that would bring the kidnapper and Amy into view. The locker door squeaked when she opened it. Lifting the heavy duffle bag to the locker, she bent over and acted as though she were transferring money inside. After shutting the locker, she again scrutinized the ticket booths, the tall windows, facing the front and reaching to the high ceiling, and doors leading to the departing buses.

She viewed the large stone pillars and hid behind one. The room spun in front of her like a merry-go-round with different riders at each turn. She grabbed the post with both arms to stop her dizziness. A boy and his father ran through the back aisle to a bus with its motor rumbling. Helen could see through the window that buses were leaving. Inside, the depot had cleared out except for a group of soldiers and those riders who were running to catch their buses.

A stout man wearing large horn-rimmed sunglasses that covered most of his face, a mustache, a dirty cap on his head, and shorts that revealed his muscular legs walked up to the locker, opened the door, and slammed it shut. "What the hell?" he exclaimed as he hit the already closed door, sending off a tinny ring. Helen knew she should wait until he calmed down, but her need to search for Amy forced her to step out. She looked around the depot, scanning every corner, but Amy was not there.

Helen strode within a few feet of the man.

"Where is my daughter?" she demanded to know.

"I told you I'd call ya," he growled.

"Where is she?" Helen knew she was doing the wrong thing but she couldn't stop.

"Listen, bitch. You give me the money or you'll never see your daughter again."

Helen's pulse pounded in her ears. "How do I know she is all right?"

"You gonna need to believe me, or else."

"You don't scare me. No daughter, no money," Helen said, squeezing her hands to stop them from shaking.

"You little bitch," he said as he reached for her. Helen clutched her bag tighter, not that she cared about the money at this point, but because it was the only hope she had of getting Amy. Helen scooted between groups of travelers, in spaces too narrow for the crook. Her back ached from the weight of the cash-filled bag.

She ran out to the garage where she scurried between buses that faced the street. The kidnapper had gained on her and she could feel his breath on her neck. She hopped on a bus, having no idea where it would go. Pain settled in her shoulders, too. The squeak of her pursuer's shoes sounded behind her. She ran to the rear door and jumped off the bus as the driver revved up the motor. Exhaust smoke flew up her nostrils and made her cough, but she kept running out onto the sidewalk. A huge hand came from behind and yanked her bag. She squeezed her arms against her body and clung to the bag so hard that her fingers turned white.

"Look, lady," he said, his breath exuding garlic. "The sooner you give me the money, the sooner you see your daughter."

He had almost convinced Helen to give in. "Is she in your car? All you have to do is show her to me and I'll give you the money."

Helen felt the blow before she looked down and saw his fat hands on her shoulders and her bag flying as her body hovered over the steamy sidewalk. The garbage can odor of dirty concrete rose to meet her as her arms and legs slapped the sidewalk. Pain seared through her as she lay on the ground, watching the worn-down heels of this terrible man become smaller as he pounded away.

Words floated on air. "FBI. Halt. Halt or we'll shoot."

Helen moved her head to see men in FBI jackets running, their guns pointed straight ahead. Onlookers backed away. Police officers ushered them across the street. *It's about time,* she thought, though she said nothing. How could she? This was her fault for ignoring their instructions and challenging the kidnapper. Her hands burned as she pushed them on the sidewalk to pull herself up. Her right leg wobbled and she tried to balance with her left. Pain like little knives rushed up and down both legs. She looked down to see blood gushing from her knees and saturating her skirt. The kidnapper was running back towards her. She tried to run. But before she could move his rough hands gripped her neck. Any minute she would be dead. She coughed. This was it. She was going to die. She stamped her heel on his toes. Pain jabbed her knee. Sun flickered on a knife blade as it moved closer toward her neck and then out of sight. The cold metal scratched her skin. Was he going to cut her neck and let her bleed to death?

"Now do as I say or you're dead." He turned halfway around, placing her in the path of the agents' guns. Walking backward, he dragged her away from the agents. Her heels scuffed the cement, creating a rhythm like the music in movies about the guillotine. She might as well have been hanging with a noose around her neck.

"Release her or we'll shoot," a man said. It sounded like Dan.

Sun danced off the blade as the kidnapper swished it towards the agents and back on her neck again. *Don't shoot*, Helen thought. They would never find Amy if they killed him. The click of their rifles' safety lever rang through the silence. The kidnapper exuded the odor of stale deodorant and sweat. At least he was frightened, but he didn't let go. How long would it be until they actually pulled the trigger? She spoke rapidly. "It's not too late. I really want to give you the money but I have to know Amy is all right."

He yanked the bag from her.

"Do you have any children, or nieces and nephews?" she asked, trying to make a last ditch plea for his sympathy. "How would you feel if you lost one of them?"

"Shut up. You're gonna help me get out of here."

Helen felt him tug her and tried to plant her feet. It was impossible. It must have been ninety degrees but her body shivered. A bullet whizzed within a millimeter of her, close enough to cause her ears to ring. The man slouched to the ground, pulling Helen with him. Instantly her nostrils filled with the dank smell of wet cotton, the sour smell of blood. Was that what death smelled like? Yes, he was dead. His lips were slack and his eyes, wide open, looked at nothing. Dan and the other agents approached the body.

"How could you kill him? Now I'll never see Amy again." Helen knew she had bungled her side of the deal, but her nerves tingled like an electrical shock.

"We'll find her," Dan said.

"How? Just tell me how, right now."

Dan scowled. "You were in imminent danger. We saved your life."

"I'd rather be dead than live without Amy." Helen's head buzzed. The agents, the cars and trees all faded. She felt as though she were floating. Then nothing.

She woke up on a gurney. For a minute, she thought she had fallen off the ship like Erich, who had been killed. An ambulance and a strange station wagon, with letters on the panel, spelling *Coroner,* were parked in the street. She pulled a plastic mask from her face, wiggled her arm out of the blood-pressure cuff, and sat up. Her knees were bandaged.

"What have you done to me?"

"Wait a minute," Dan said. "You just passed out. They're going to take you to the hospital for observation."

"I'll be fine. It's not every day I see someone next to me die from a bullet." Saying that took every ounce of strength that Helen had. But she had to act calm to get rid of everyone so she could figure out how to find out where Amy was being held.

Dan huddled with the ambulance attendants and returned to Helen. "I'll take you home," he offered.

All the way back to her apartment, Helen kept her eyes closed. She didn't want to talk to Dan. She was afraid of her anger, and also afraid she would say something to encourage him to come inside with her. When he parked the car in front of the apartment, she stretched as though she were waking from a nap.

"I'll go in with you and speak with the agent," he said before he stepped out of the car and opened the passenger door. He looked at her legs and put his arm around her waist. "Lean on me," he said as he led her to the apartment building.

"There's no need for you to come inside. I'm really tired and I'm going to take a nap," Helen said, telling herself that this wasn't a lie because she had considered resting later.

"I won't bother you. I just want to check on our operations."

Grudgingly Helen let him help her into the apartment, though she could have managed on her own. Once Dan and the technician were involved in their whispered conversation, she poured boiling water into a cup and swished the teabag in circles like a fortune teller divining a location for Amy. The technician's voice came to mind. After the kidnapper's call, the technician had mentioned that the call probably came from Northeast Portland between 33rd and 41st sStreets. She knew the area well because she had attended school there. Even so, there were lots of cros-streets and he hadn't mentioned any of them. Well, she would look until she found something.

By the time Dan left, it was late afternoon and too dark for Helen to accomplish anything. Somehow she would get away to search the area first thing the next morning when it was light.

Chapter Seventeen

The sleeping pill that Helen had finally decided to use had worked for a few hours. She woke up and glanced at Amy's bed. The quilt was flat. It was a quilt that Helen had bought at Meier and Frank's department store. Amy loved the print with huge shoes and little children climbing all over them. She insisted Helen have one just like it. When Helen had tucked her into bed Amy would recite: *Little old woman lived in a shoe. She had so many children she didn't know what to do.*

Amy had asked her if she was going to have lots of children and Helen had answered, "No, because I have you and no one can be as special as you." The memory of Amy's laughter rang in Helen's ears. She looked at the bed again. Amy was missing. Would she ever see her again? Tears gushed down her cheeks.

She heard the clatter of dishes in the kitchen. The clock on the table said 6:30. Her skin prickled. Had the kidnappers come after her? She glanced around the room for a weapon and grabbed the table lamp before she remembered that the technician who had tapped the phone had slept on the sofa. She put down the lamp, threw on her chenille robe, and padded her bare feet into the front area.

Helen expected to see the young technician and had to look twice before she realized that Dan was standing near the drain board. Strands of his crew-cut hair poked in all directions. He flashed a half-smile and shrugged his shoulders. He looked like a little boy with a secret. "I brought some cinnamon rolls," Don said rapidly as though eager to explain his presence. "The coffee will be ready in a minute."

"Thank you." Helen couldn't think of anything else to say. She ran her hand through her hair. It was a mess but she didn't care. Dan reached over and wiped a tear from her face.

She ran into the bathroom and brushed her teeth to get rid of the stale taste in her mouth. The tang of Ipana toothpaste refreshed her.

In her bedroom, she was halfway into her coveralls when Dan called to her: "I told your boss you wouldn't be in today."

Suddenly, her gratitude turned to resentment. How dare he speak for her like that? What did he really know of what she was going through? He had no idea what a mother felt about losing her child, maybe forever. Helen squeezed her eyes shut for a second. There was no time for emotions. She had to find a way to escape from Dan.

She should have interviewed the staff at the Vanport Kindergarten more thoroughly before sending Amy there. Those teachers had neglected Amy. Helen's guilt stifled her. Finding Amy would make up for such carelessness. Helen slipped into a skirt and blouse and joined Dan in the front room. Once the technician came, she would need to sneak past him, which would be easier than getting rid of Dan. When evening came it would be too difficult to locate the kidnapper's hiding place. She knew better than to tell Dan about her plans and stretched the truth for Amy's sake. "I have a job to do at the shipyard. How long are you going to keep me away?"

He thrust his jaw in what Helen saw as a professional mode. "Until we find your daughter."

"That's ridiculous," Helen said without thinking. "I mean, people will tell me things that they wouldn't tell you."

Dan's ears turned red. "I know you're upset so I'll ignore what you said."

Encouraged by his slight concession, Helen decided to try again. "My baby is out there somewhere and I need to find her."

"Leave that to us," Dan said. "I'll be working with an agent from Violent Crimes."

"Crimes," Helen said. She knew that taking Amy was a crime, but *violent* made her mind race to all kinds of rapes and murders. "What will happen to Amy?" she asked, not really wanting to know the answer, at least not if it involved violent crimes.

"We're working on finding her. The technician will stay here to listen in on your phone when calls come in."

"*If* a call comes." Helen struggled to hold back the tears, which were ready to burst. She had thought that she would never eat again, but the pungent scent of cinnamon mesmerized her. She took a bite and imagined it was a magic drug, which would put her to sleep and when she woke up Amy would be home.

Dan fixed his eyes on her. "Have you heard from your husband? Our agents in California are staking out his house in Atherton and say he's not at home."

Edgar's angry face floated in Helen's mind. She took a sip of coffee. "The last time I saw him was at the market. He was staying at the Multnomah Hotel. When I called they said he had checked out."

"I'll alert our Bureau," Dan said.

"Edgar's a vindictive man. Just to get back at me, to make sure I didn't end up happy, he could've taken Amy. But it didn't sound like she was with anyone she knew when I talked to her on the phone. And besides, he adores Amy and wouldn't put her through the trauma." Helen suspected that Dan was not being realistic because he resented Edgar, was maybe even a little jealous of him. Certainly, Dan had shown feelings for her. "If Edgar was the one to take her, then why would he need a dog? Dog. If only I had bought Amy a dog." Helen's chest caved in and her sobs rushed out.

"He could have hired someone to abduct her for him."

Helen realized that she had overreacted about Don letting his feelings for her influence his judgment of Edgar. She took deep breaths to calm herself. Given the time necessary to get rid of Dan, the day would be half gone. "I have a job to do at the shipyard. How long are you going to keep me away?"

"Until we find your daughter."

Helen stared at her half-eaten cinnamon roll. She should never have become attracted to Dan. He was loyal to the FBI and stuck in their protocol. She couldn't accept his devotion to the Agency when her daughter's life was at stake. And if their relationship developed further after Amy was found, would she want to constantly compete with the FBI? "I'm going to go nuts inside the house all day."

"I'll take you any place you want to go."

"The shipyard," she said to taunt him.

"That's not funny." Dan bent over Helen and kissed her forehead. He acted as if this were normal, so much so that she almost felt that it was, in spite of the chemistry that charged between them when his lips made contact with her skin. "I wish you would take the danger you're in seriously."

Helen forced herself to ignore the electricity his kiss gave her. "My baby is missing. *That* is serious."

To distract herself, Helen phoned her mother. Being really desperate to escape Dan's supervision, she invited her to have lunch in the Meier and Franks Tearoom. Her mother was delighted, which made Helen feel like a worm. Helen grasped *The Saturday Evening Post* from her bedside table and studied Rosie's confident face, drawing strength from the defiance in her eyes and tilted chin. What would Rosie do in this situation? She would find her child. That is what Helen would do, too. Maybe she could run her own investigation. She took one more look at Rosie and knew she could do that.

From the footlocker under her bed, she took a linen dress, pumps, a pillbox hat, and white gloves, which she had thought she would never wear again. She told Dan about the plan to meet her mother.

"Great," he said, grinning. "I'll drive you there."

"I can drive. You don't want to wait while I change my clothes. Besides, how will I get home?" Helen knew she had him because he had to work.

"I'll pick you up." He might as well have said, *Gotcha.*

Chapter Eighteen

When they arrived at the department store, Helen took pleasure from stepping out of the car before Dan could come to help her. His attentiveness was starting to make her feel claustrophobic, like surveillance. She and her mother met on the main floor, under the clock that looked like a pocket watch. Her mother's slate-gray dress draped from the large shoulder pads down her corseted body.

"What are the authorities doing?" her mother asked, her cheeks flushing like two ripe plums. "Are they giving Amy's disappearance enough attention?"

"Of course they are," Helen said, only to ease her mother's concern. She moved towards the elevator and turned to make sure that her mother had followed her. They took the elevator to the top floor where the tearoom was located. Helen's pumps sunk into the deep carpeting as she followed her mother past the heavy drapes that hung over the floor-to-ceiling windows like dark clouds. The room smelled of peppermint, ginger, and lavender perfume. Light from the crystal chandeliers bounced off the metal bars on the uniforms of Army and Navy officers who sat with wives or mothers. Her mother stopped at every table to greet friends, who smiled through the checkered veils on their hats. With all the time this took, Helen was afraid she would lose her nerve. The plan to deceive her mother had been a last resort and made Helen nervous enough without a delay. They finally sat at the linen-clad table.

The waitress came to take their orders. She wore a black dress with a white organza apron and white nurses' shoes. Helen ordered a crab salad and coffee without looking at the menu. Her mother studied every listing and finally ordered the same thing.

While they were waiting for their food, her mother said, "I feel horrified by what has happened to you. Please let me help. You seem to pull away when you really need someone. If only you would come home, it would make your life easier and it would be nice for me because your father is away."

Helen couldn't answer. This was the first time her mother had been direct about her feelings, rather than lecturing. If the waitress hadn't brought the food, Helen would probably have accepted her offer. The avocado melted on her tongue as she chewed the chunky crab. She wished they could just be having lunch, that this were a normal day and that her child was safely at school instead of missing. Her mother had appeared to be sincere. Helen considered dropping her plans to borrow the car.

"Where's Dad?"

Her mother wiped her lips with a linen napkin. "He is back in Washington."

"I thought the senate was on summer recess."

"Oh, Honey, I hate to burden you with this when you have suffered so much already with the kidnapping. President Roosevelt has slapped your father's face, ignoring his appeal for help with Uncle Aaron."

The words were like a lasso, pulling her away from her plans to question people at the shipyard. Helen couldn't deceive her mother like this. But she had to. By the time she would catch the next bus to Vanport, the day would be gone and she wouldn't have time to question anyone or do a little snooping. She could drive to the shipyard, check on some workers, and return her mother's car. She needed the key.

"Uncle Aaron? That is so sad," she finally managed to say as she imagined Rosie's portrait to give her strength. Amy's life was at stake. Helen's jaw ached from clenching as she bent down and fiddled with her shoe with one hand while the other slid into her mother's purse to retrieve the keys.

Her mother's whisper sounded like a hiss. "What on earth are you doing?"

"My shoe slipped off my foot and I couldn't find it." Faking the need for a handkerchief, she dropped the stolen item into her own purse. Yes, she considered it stolen. Now she was a liar and a thief. Jewelry and officers' bars sent dots around the room like the vision spots of a migraine headache as Helen sat back in her chair. She grasped the table to prevent herself from falling. After she found Amy, maybe they would move in with her parents.

Once she steadied her body, she took another bite of avocado. It stuck in her throat. "Excuse me, I need to visit the ladies' room," she called, already on her way. As she walked inside the lounge, large flowers on the wallpaper danced in front of her eyes. She took a deep breath and stopped at the basins, where she splashed cold water on her face. Six girls were gathered nearby. It occurred to Helen that her mother could decide to join her in the powder room. If so, how would she get out unnoticed?

"We're late," the tallest girl said. The rest of them all spoke at once. "Gregory Peck won't get there until all the bands have played and they have sold the bonds."

Helen knew they were talking about the War Bond Rally. She recalled the actor's dark hair and throaty voice and insinuated herself in the middle of the group. "I just love him." At least that was the truth. When no one invited her to join them she took six dollar bills out of her wallet and spoke in a *just-us-girls* voice, which she called up from her past. "My ex-boyfriend has been following me everywhere. Here's a dollar for each one of you to make sure he doesn't see me."

They each took a bill and laughed. The tall girl said, "Here, wear my jacket until we get out of the building. Colleen, give your hat to this woman."

Helen looked in the mirror. With the hat's huge rim pulled down over her forehead and the cotton jacket falling below her knees and covering most of her arms, she didn't recognize herself. Linking arms, the girls formed a shield around her as they walked to the escalator. "This is so exciting," one of the girls said as they all ran down the escalator steps, faster than it could move them. On the other side of the store they took an elevator to the ground floor and exited.

Chapter Nineteen

With drivers looking for parking spaces and pedestrians pushing their way to the event, Helen feared she would never get to the Packard. She took deep breaths to relax. Walter Pigeon, the movie actor, was already on the stage. It was 104 degrees and people were crushed close together. They must have been scalding, packed that tight, dressed in too many layers of clothes while the sun scorched their heads and shoulders. Helen saw one person faint and saw a nurse running toward the body.

With the girls, Helen finally made it across the street. In front of the car, she returned the jacket and hat and hastened into the driver's seat.

"Good luck," the girls said in chorus.

The traffic made Helen dizzy. She swung the Packard out and joined the throng of cars. It could probably take her mother about fifteen minutes to become concerned about Helen and to notice her keys missing and then her car. Once Helen had driven several blocks, the traffic flowed slightly faster. She was almost to the bridge on-ramp when she noticed a black-and-white car in her rearview mirror. She took a sudden turn to the right. Horns honked. The car, which was definitely police, followed. *Darn it.* Helen thought she had more time. Her mother must have alerted the entire police force.

By the time she reached Broadway Street, where she had planned to lose her pursuer in traffic, his red and white lights flashed across her mirror and bounced off the dashboard. Helen edged in between two cars, hoping to lose him. He answered her attempt with his siren. She turned left up 6th Street and then took a sharp right. It was no use. He was right behind her. Her sweaty hands slid all over the steering wheel. She grasped it tightly until her fingers throbbed and steered to the curb. Darn it. How was she going to find Amy?

The officer loomed over her. Black stubble covered the skin above his lips and on his chin. "Step out of the car, miss."

"What did I do wrong, Officer?" Helen asked.

"Step out of the car," he said, more forcefully. As she stepped down onto the pavement, she noticed another policeman slide in behind the Packard's steering wheel. "Wait a minute. This is my mother's car."

"Yes, and it has been reported stolen."

"Just call my mother. She'll tell you it's okay." Helen was startled when he grabbed her arm and shoved her into the back of his car. "Call my mother and tell her it's me. I use her car often."

He closed the door, locked it from the outside and proceeded to the driver's seat. "Nope. She's pressing charges." He laughed again, a loud, raucous exclamation.

Helen wanted to say: *Listen, you jerk, I may be small and I may be a woman but I work at the shipyard.* She softened her statement. "I know you'll understand. I weld ships for our victory and was just trying to get to work. Men's lives depend on me."

He laughed so hard he started coughing. When he recovered, he flashed his lights to ease into the traffic. "And right now you're under arrest."

For the rest of the ride, Helen closed her eyes and imagined reaching over and twisting his neck until the bones broke. When they arrived at the courthouse, the officer grasped her arm with more pressure than necessary, and led her up the steps and along the marble floor to the judge's office.

Her mother sat in an upholstered chair across from the judge. When she saw Helen, she cried, "How could you do this to me?"

She watched the drops run down her mother's face. "Mother, I'm so sorry to upset you. I needed to get to work and find out who took Amy."

"You could have asked me."

"You're right, I should have." Helen said, though she knew her mother would have insisted that Helen leave this to the authorities. Would she actually let them arrest her?

Chapter Twenty

D an sat at the long table in the conference room and rubbed his neck with his fingers, trying to massage away the knot caused from bending over his records with Albert and the chiefs of their two divisions, not to mention the strain of dealing with Helen. With his other hand, he passed the mimeographed bios of his murder suspects across the maple table to the men.

"Jason from Espionage will be here soon to describe the spy activities," Dan said.

"He's late," the chief complained.

Dan noticed the other men folding and unfolding their hands while they sat rigidly on the tall chairs. To calm them down, he modulated his voice and said, "Their chief is on vacation and they are short-handed. He'll be here soon."

Albert shuffled through the printout, holding it as though he had found a dead rat. "As of now, we are centering on the shipyard or someone with close connections. No one saw a car where the dogs acted on the victim's scent and it concerns me that it could be an outside job."

Dan glanced at the innocuous photographs on the pale walls and thought that the room was as unrevealing as the conversation. The unread printouts sat stiffly where they had been placed. Dan decided to infuse some life into the meeting and answered Albert's comment.

"Don't you have that backwards? If no car was seen, then it had to be someone who was already inside or at least could enter without causing any alarm. And they had to know their way around." Dan felt shame for the joy that he experienced from disagreeing with Albert.

The chief said, "We're approaching twenty-four hours, and the statistical likelihood of finding her alive is decreasing by the second. We've got to have something almost immediately."

Dan knew that, but it chilled him to hear someone else remind him of the odds. "Albert, you can come with me to the shipyards this afternoon, if you wish, and we can question some workers as well as check their backgrounds more carefully." He would never have invited Albert to join him if the chief hadn't been there. Dan wished he could overcome his need to impress the chief.

A man knocked on the door and entered the room. Dan recognized Ray Gardner, a skinny guy with a circle of gray hair around a bald scalp.

"We're ready to hear from you," the chief said.

Ray loomed above the other agents, even when he sat down. He placed a pile of papers on the table and shuffled through them. He cleared his throat before he spoke. "These are copies of letters returned as Return to Sender. We know the dead man and his wife owned a doll shop. Upon interviewing the recipients, it's clear they all shop at the International Doll Shop on 5th and Alder. It appears someone has appropriated their addresses from the store records."

"That sounds familiar," Albert said as he picked a sheet of paper from his stack and concentrated on it. "Just as I thought. The Yamamoto woman owned the shop."

"I don't think so," Ray said. "She was a former owner before this spying began.

"Let's go," Dan said. "We can double-check her background at the shipyard."

The chief intervened. "Not so fast. Your witness is downstairs in Judge Lakin's office. She stole her mother's car. You better get on down there now."

"Is she all right?" Dan asked, feeling a mixture of worry and anger.

"She's fine but she ran us a merry chase."

For a second the seriousness of this case receded as he pictured Helen being arrested. He admired her spunk but she scared him. He understood how desperate she was to find her child, which had no doubt wiped out her ability to judge the danger she put herself in by doing something so reckless as auto theft.

Helen was seated facing the judge's desk, her shoulders hunched. He felt a surge of mixed emotions, none professional, which alarmed him. He had let his personal emotions get in the way of his job. He had fallen for Helen and he felt sorry for her. But anger boiled inside him because she had gone off on her own.

"I am releasing this woman to you. She needs constant attention." The judge sounded eager to get rid of Helen.

"That's exactly what I intend to give her, your honor," Dan said as he approached Helen. On the way to the car, he glanced at Helen's defiant eyes, the curve of her breasts, and her tiny waist. His heart thudded. He struggled to sound stern when he said, "I could have told you that car theft wouldn't help you."

"Have you found Amy?"

"Not yet," Dan admitted as he pulled the car out of the parking lot.

"I'll find her," Helen said between sobs. "I'll figure out something. I have to."

Dan felt like a heel. His profession didn't allow for personal feelings, but anyone would be moved by a mother's loss of a child. He tried to tell himself that this was all he was feeling, that it wasn't Helen in particular who was getting into his heart.

"Listen," he said quickly. "I'm going to take you to the shipyard because I don't know what else to do with you. I'm going to check if anyone has missed work since yesterday."

"That's what I wanted to do in the first place," Helen said.

As they approached the ship, Dan noticed the large number of workers, some walking around and others wielding tools. How was he going to protect Helen and get his work done? He had been weak in letting her influence him to bring her.

When he was first assigned to the shipyard, Dan had felt honored. He would be helping the war effort. Espionage had always excited him and he couldn't wait to get into the thick of it. So far, he had squashed a few spy activities in which the spies were incompetent, babysat President Roosevelt when Eleanor had christened a ship, and now he was emotionally involved in a kidnap case.

Chapter Twenty-one

Helen felt a sense of welcome mixed with apprehension. The shipyard was where she worked, but the work she did there, the connections she had made, had indirectly resulted in the disappearance of her daughter. The ground was damp from the night before. Sun poked through the clouds, which cast a steamy heat. The air smelled of damp leaves, at once fresh and dank; the bumps on the stucco buildings floated like specks of sugar.

She walked up the steps with Dan behind her. Whatever fear she had of climbing up there had disappeared. She was Rosie the Riveter looking for her daughter.

They walked along the deck past Helen's station. A woman she didn't recognize was doing Helen's job. This made her feel cheated, though she knew this was unrealistic. She was too emotional to work, and no one here was irreplaceable. That was the nature of the assembly line.

Dan led her to the center of the deck. Charlotte was up on top of the deckhouse, as usual. When she saw Helen, she ran down the ladder and reached her arms to hug her. Dan stepped between them, his hand on his gun. He shoved Charlotte aside, leaving a scent of her lavender cologne.

"For Heaven's sake," Helen said, barely able to speak. "What are you doing? She's my friend."

"That's all right," Charlotte said. "I understand. This is just horrible.

Do you have any idea who did such a disgusting thing?"

"We're working on it," Dan said before speaking to Helen. "You stay right here where I can see you. I'm going to talk to the supervisor."

While Helen watched, Dan gathered all the lead men and spoke, his voice so low she couldn't make out the words. The men mumbled to each other and one of them spoke clearly: "Trudy Grant quit because cleaning was too hard for her; that work's a bitch. Mike Johnson, a pipe fitter, has four days off and is fishing in Astoria. Janet Mason had accumulated a week off and stayed at home, I think. She's an electrician."

Dan thanked them, put his arm around Helen, and led her to the stairs.

Ordinarily, this would have excited her but she felt only flushes of anger about the way he had treated Charlotte. "How could you be so rude to Charlotte? You're ten times larger than she is."

"Everyone is a suspect until we find Amy."

"Charlotte?"

Dan didn't answer her.

When they reached the administration building, given the way he had reacted to the embrace with Charlotte, Helen cautiously edged toward Roxanne, whom she saw seated behind an oak desk in the cubicle outside the executive's office for Public Relations.

When Roxanne saw Helen, the rapid click of typewriter keys subsided and Roxanne scooted out of her chair. A light blue maternity smock silhouetted her pregnant body. She appeared to enjoy the obviousness of her pregnancy, flaunting her condition. Helen felt like socking her in the stomach. My God, was she so distraught over Amy that she would deny anyone happiness? Of course she wouldn't harm Roxanne, but wished the future mother would be subtle about her condition. Helen knew that her own reaction was a product of frayed nerves.

"I am so sorry about your daughter," Roxanne said as she pulled the plastic cover over her typewriter. "Any leads?"

Helen was startled for a second, even suspicious, until she reasoned that the news of the kidnap was everywhere. The FBI had even distributed posters from the pictures Helen had furnished. "The FBI is working on it and I have to hope they'll find her."

Roxanne thought for a minute. "Who do they think took her?"

"Do you have any information?"

Roxanne laughed nervously. "Heavens, I have no idea."

Helen sensed that Roxanne was hiding something. Or, was it just her stupidity and the embarrassment of not understanding the situation?

"Have you seen any suspicious-looking strangers around the yard?"

Roxanne squinted at Helen. "What do you mean?"

She was either a good actress or dumber than Helen thought.

Chapter Twenty-two

At the administration building, Dan left Helen, talking to Roxanne and joined Albert. The two men headed for the records department. The room was larger than a football field, with rows of file cabinets lined up against the wall. The vastness discouraged Dan. He read and memorized the files of the absent workers that the lead men had mentioned. Albert read them three more times and was still arranging them precisely in the center of the table for discussion.

Dan realized his own tendency to work speedily and tried to control his impatience. Finally he said, "I think I better go check on Helen."

"Are you two a couple?" Albert asked.

Dan's face flushed. "She's my witness and the kidnapped child's mother. She could be in danger."

Albert smiled. "She's very attractive."

Dan thought about her red hair, her eyes the color of jade. "I guess she is."

"In our work, it's been my experience to be exceedingly cautious about women. Especially attractive women connected to investigations."

Dan felt his face burn and figured his cheeks were bright red. He laughed. The tone of his laughter surprised him. It had an edge to it and was a dead giveaway. But this was none of Albert's business.

"If you want to move ahead in the Bureau," Albert continued, "maybe be a chief one day, getting involved with a divorcée could lead to wedding bells and snuff out any chance of a promotion."

"Marriage? Are you nuts? I barely know her and I'm not going down that road again," Dan said. He shoved his chair back and walked down the hall to find Helen.

She seemed happy to see him. "I want to look up someone's address."

"That's easy enough," Dan said, relieved that she had calmed down. "I'm headed for the records room right now."

When they reached the room, Albert said, "Nothing alarming here. Did you know that Johnson, the dead guy, has a wife working in the yard? Betty Johnson."

"Betty?" Helen asked. "The guy who kidnapped Amy is Betty's husband?"

"I questioned her after he was killed," Dan said, still angry with Albert. "She's an electrician."

Albert came right back at him. "You questioned an obvious suspect without including me? You broke protocol."

Albert was right. Dan apologized. "I had to act immediately before she found out about her husband's death." He loosened his tie, partly in contrast to Albert's precise tie-knot and partly because he knew Albert was right about protocol and because he was uncomfortable with Helen and Albert in the same room, given Albert's derision of Helen, his comments about how attractive she was, and his suspicion that Dan liked her.

Dan forced himself to concentrate on working his way out of this diversion. "Betty Johnson wasn't aware of her husband's actions and there was no way to connect her. We have surveillance on their house."

"Our kidnapper was caught and killed, as you well know," Albert said, obviously unable to forgive Dan for excluding him.

"Someone has the child." Dan was annoyed at this waste of time. "We should check all of these people who had missed work at the time of the kidnapping. I'll get their addresses for our surveillance crews."

As Dan would have expected, Albert ignored Helen and directed his attention to Dan. "I read your report on the killing of Erich Cranston and all of the suspects. The only suspect I can consider is the Yamamoto woman. She has the International Doll Shop on 5th and Alder.

"Erich's wife bought it from her," Helen said.

Helen was more positive than Ray about the ownership and Dan wondered if she had sensed Albert's disdain and was therefore showing off. "Are you sure?"

"I saw her at the shipyard and the other women told me. Charlotte was standing right there."

Albert had that dog fetching a bone look on his face. "Yamamoto could still be involved."

Instead of arguing with him, Dan directed his question to Helen. "Do you know anything about Charlotte that would point to criminal activity?"

"Erich's widow has been running the shop since the Japanese bombed Pearl Harbor." Helen didn't know what else to say. Her instinct was to protect Charlotte until she realized that whoever took Amy could be connected to the spying. "I really don't know."

Albert persevered. "Now think carefully here. Have you noticed Yamamoto acting strangely?"

Charlotte glared at Albert. "Her name is Charlotte."

"Okay," Albert said, his lips protruding like a dog ready to attack. "Charlotte, or anyone else acting strangely?"

Helen looked at Dan. "I can't stand this anymore. Shouldn't you be out searching for the missing workers and finding Amy?"

Once they had left Albert behind, Helen reached inside her purse and retrieved the letter to show Dan.

You still owe me $3,000.00 per our purchase agreement.
If I do not receive it by end of month, I will contact my lawyer.

He read it quickly. "How did you get this? On second thought, I don't want to know."

"It makes Charlotte sound guilty, doesn't it?" Helen wanted him to disagree with her.

As usual, he was neutral. "I'll take the note to the lab. Maybe the technician can find fingerprints other than the ones you left."

Helen decided not to wait any longer to find out if Charlotte might have Amy. She couldn't believe her good luck. Dan appeared to be preoccupied with getting back to the Bureau. All she had to do was wait for Dan to leave, which he did sooner than she had feared.

Her next hurdle was to jumpstart her car, since she couldn't alert the technician by getting her backup key. This was something she had only seen others do. Hesitantly, she sat in the driver's seat of her car with no idea of where to begin. Her visor was out of whack. Helen was really annoyed with the way Dan let these guys drive her car. *It's a wonder the Chevy is in one piece.* What had this man done to it? She reached up and tried to straighten the visor. Her key dropped onto the mat. He had left the key in the car. He probably thought that the technician or Dan would be watching her.

She drove across the Burnside Bridge and over to Alder and up to 5th, where she parked across the street from the International Doll Shop. She slid down in her seat until only her eyes were level with the bottom of the window.

The woman she had seen at the shipyard walked down 5th, as confident as the other time Helen had seen her, and entered the shop. Helen already knew the woman owned the store. This was a wild goose chase. Even so, Helen waited and watched.

When she was ready to give up, the store's door swung open and Charlotte walked out to the curb.

While Charlotte was looking left and right, a sure sign she would cross the street, Helen steered her car out of the parking place and sped down 5th until she turned onto Broadway, passing the Paramount and Orpheum theatres and the Oregon Journal building, all familiar, which calmed Helen enough to interpret what she had seen. Charlotte was still involved with the doll shop or she could have been shopping or simply curious. Helen tried to dismiss the idea that Charlotte might be in on the spy scheme, but the suspicion nagged at her.

When she arrived home, the technician met her at the door. "You gave us all a scare."

"Did I get any phone calls?"

"No, but you could have."

Helen went to her room. She didn't need to be lectured by that kid. It would be bad enough when she discussed her fears about Charlotte with Dan.

Chapter Twenty-three

The next morning, Helen woke early and didn't allow herself to think about anything except finding where Amy had been hidden. After the fiasco with her mother's car, Helen decided to drive her own Chevy to the location the technician had mentioned. She dressed quietly in a pair of trousers and a T-shirt and slipped her feet into a pair of Keds, which she laced up with a double knot. She was pleased that the pain in her legs had subsided. Careful to avoid making any noise, she slid the window open and scooted out.

When she reached 33rd, Helen drove past colonial houses with green shutters, one of which was where Freddy Gristle had lived. Her mother had insisted she date him because his mother was her friend. Helen remembered her one and only date with him at Jantzen Beach Ballroom. His feet had seemed to stick to the floor; they moved like a car with a bad clutch. Before long, she was leading him, the way she had led the boys at Mr. Billings' dance class. He danced so close his sweat dripped on her neck and the dark fuzz on his chin tickled her forehead. She kept her eyes on the floor so she wouldn't see any of the popular kids she knew. That was a long time ago and seemed even longer since the search for Amy had wiped out any superficial concerns. Was God punishing her for past behavior?

She continued on past large wood or brick houses with pitched roofs, bordered by rose bushes and trimmed hedges. At every house, bicycles and cars were parked in driveways: family homes where a neighbor would know if a kidnapper had brought a strange child into a house. She continued driving until the houses turned into small wood bungalows with brown spots on the lawns. Maybe in this neighborhood, she thought. But the houses were closer together and parents and children sat on front porches.

This was hopeless. She was not going to find Amy here, and she was stupid to try this without help or more information. She headed towards the bridge and home. As she crossed a small overpass, Helen noticed a patch of wild weeds and small box-like houses, some with doors falling off hinges and others with faded wood slabs that were chipped. She recognized the area as Sullivan's Gulch.

One of her friends in high school had lived there, and Helen's mother had told her she should not associate with such people. Helen had been fascinated with that family. Gloria was in charge of her two sisters and four brothers because her mother worked, coming home just in time to cook dinner. The children wandered through the house, happily wearing worn-out, mismatched shirts and pants. Even when their mother was home, she never told them to change their clothes or to stand up straight. Helen had imagined she lived in their house and that she wore stained shorts and a sloppy blouse and lay on her bed reading all day without being told she was lazy.

Pete, the oldest boy, had been teaching Helen to pass a football until James, his younger brother, lay down in the street to prove that God was watching out for him and nothing would hurt him. After a truck's wheels crunched James' leg so badly the bones stuck out of his knee, Helen could not go near their house again.

She re-crossed the overpass and parked her car. Returning to the gulch, she walked along the strawlike grass and weeds that reminded her of cockleburs from a fairy tale. Most of the hovels looked as though no one lived in them. Amy could be inside or could be rotting away. No, Helen refused to consider such a possibility.

She counted the hodgepodge of shacks. There were five very close together. Dried weeds crowded the wood. It took no time at all to go through the open shacks. The smell of beer and urine made bile come up in her throat. This was useless but she knew there was no choice but to continue searching. Helen didn't remember the area being this bad when she had gone to Gloria's house after school.

Helen approached one of the larger dwellings. Standing out against the brown-spotted weeds was a swatch of fabric, torn from a garment. She bent to observe the material. Amy's polka-dot bow? There were lots of bows like that. But this one seemed to hit her in the eyes. She wanted to bend down and inhale the bow, but the ground spun around her. She dug her feet into the dirt to avoid falling. Did the kidnapper knock Amy down, or did he drag her roughly?

The front of the building consisted of several panels. She pressed her ear against the wood. The absence of voices or movement created silence, a warning of trouble, like the lull before a storm. Helen shivered. She shoved at the thin wood and found that it was stronger than it looked. She pulled weeds under the outside wall, faster and faster. Pain shot through her legs but she refused to stop. Amy could be inside. Helen's hands were scratched raw. Wiggling her body underneath, she entered the abomination. In the front room, a mattress with worn blankets lay on the floor. A small camping stove sat on a makeshift counter next to a miniscule sink.

Helen moved to the rest of what used to be a house. The floor planks squeaked as her shoes pressed them. The bathroom stunk of urine. The basin was rusted and the toilet stained. Poor Amy, if this was where she had been staying.

Across from the bathroom was a closed room. Did Helen dare think that Amy was there? To avoid messing up any clues, Helen wrapped her handkerchief around her hand, opened the door and surveyed the room. Next to a bed, an orange crate substituted for a bedside table. On top of it was a small cardboard book of *Goldilocks and the Three Bears*. Amy loved that book. Thoughts of her spending time in this filthy excuse for a house set Helen's skin on fire. Amy had been here. Helen knew it. But where was she now?

Helen stared at a shower curtain substituting for a closet door. If she pulled it aside would a body fall out? *Stop this right now,* she told herself. With the same handkerchief around her hand, she pulled the curtain. She saw a blouse, turned halfway inside out, and a man's old jacket with the lining hanging from the pocket spread askew in the otherwise empty closet.

To continue her search for clues, she bent to look under the bed. Hidden partway under the metal bedpost, Helen noticed an open compact with spilled powder on the floor. Someone had been in a hurry to leave.

"Yoo hoo," a woman's voice called. "Anyone home?"

Helen struggled to breathe. Pain jabbed her chest. She ran to the window, took a deep breath and squeezed the lock. It was stuck. Sounds of the floor creaking came closer. Helen pushed her hands against the window. The glass fell out in one large piece. She jumped onto the ground. Knifelike jabs throbbed up her legs but she kept running. She saw an old Ford. What paint was left on it was black and rust had stained the rest of the car. It hadn't been there when Helen had arrived. It must have belonged to the woman whose voice she had heard.

Her hands shook while the rest of her body felt like a ghost floated inside it. She looked through the car windows. Amy was not inside and Helen didn't have any time to think. She needed to call Dan.

She drove to Kienow's Grocery Store, which was only a few blocks away. Inside she asked to use the phone. Mr. Kienow started to chat the way he always used to when Helen had come there with her mother, but when he looked at her face, he handed her the phone. She must have been a sight. No time to explain why. She dialed the FBI number, which she unfortunately knew by heart. When Dan answered, words tumbled from Helen's mouth. In some order, she gave him the location of the Gulch where a child, most likely Amy, had been. "Hurry," she repeated several times.

"Don't go inside the house. It's a crime scene and our experts know how to not disturb the evidence." His voice was a monotone, obviously intended to calm Helen, but instead it agitated her. She pictured him dragging his feet when she wanted him to run to his car.

"I'll be in front. Hurry!" Helen said before she hung up. Halfway to the door, she turned to thank Mr. Kienow.

He joined her and placed a U-no bar in her hand. "Are you all right? Can I help?"

Helen shook her head. Tears ran down her face. Every time she had come to his store, she had bought the candybar. She took a bite of the chocolate and waited for it to make her feel good the way it always had. She choked on the strong cocoa. Carefully rewrapping the bar, she told herself she would save it for Amy.

Chapter Twenty-four

Back in her room, Amy didn't know what to do. She wanted her mommy. The lady wanted to keep her. Maybe she liked her. If she liked her she wouldn't hit her.

Mommy never did that. *That mean lady can't have me*, Amy thought. Kill. She knew what kill meant. Little Orphan Annie stopped bad people. What could Amy do? She tiptoed over to the window and looked down at the brown dots of grass and bent-straw plants. Three girls were jumping rope. She knocked on the window. They waved. Amy shouted, "Help me." They waved again and went back to their jumping. She tried to undo the lock again. It wouldn't move. She pressed her face to the glass and watched her tears streak the dusty window. She knocked again. The girls picked up their ropes and walked away.

The door opened. Amy tried to run away from the window but the man took steps larger than Jack's giant after Jack had climbed the beanstalk. He grabbed the back of her dress and threw her on the bed. "You try that again and I'll throw you out the window." He smelled like the drink Daddy used to have at his cocktail hour with Mommy. His hands were larger than the giant's.

Amy promised herself she would never grab her Raggedy Ann doll again. After he left she tiptoed over to the window again and looked out to see an empty field. She rushed back to the bed and cried without making any noise. Her heart beat so hard she was afraid her body was going to burst. *Mommy, Mommy,* she whispered.

Chapter Twenty-five

Helen drove back to the Gulch and cowered inside her car, waiting for Dan. The rusted car was still in the same place. She thought about going back to the shack where she had seen the book, but was afraid the woman who had called out would still be there. She sat in the car as long as she could. Finally, she got out and crouched behind some wet cardboard soggy with coffee, chocolate, and egg yolk-colored stains. The sound of crushing weeds alerted Helen. It wasn't safe to assume the noise was Dan's car. She wanted to run but couldn't move.

He strode into her view, swinging his arms, shoulders firm, his chin thrust forward, and stood above her. He swung his arm and pointed at the area. "Seeing all of these dilapidated shacks, I tried to decide whether you are brave or just stupid to put yourself in yet another dangerous situation."

"I don't understand a word you are saying," Helen said to cover up her hurt feelings.

"Do you realize how dangerous it is for you to investigate on your own?"

"Someone had to make progress," Helen said, feeling the dampness under her eyes.

"I guess the Bureau has ignored this area," Dan said as he ran his hand through his hair. "Once the Depression was over and the homeless people had moved out of the shacks, we kind of forgot about it."

Helen tried to understand what Dan said but she could only think about him finding Amy. "I'll show you where I saw Amy's book." She shuffled through the weeds, followed by Dan, the agents from his department and those from the Evidence Response Team.

They went to the house where Helen had found the book, but this time, instead of crawling under the wall, the agents chopped an opening in the wood. Helen stopped suddenly and pointed at the dirt. "Amy's blue and white polka dot ribbon. The same place as it was before," she said, her voice becoming desperate. Her arm arched with the desire to grab the ribbon. Helen remembered Amy had worn it the day she was kidnapped. It matched the blue pinafore she had chosen to wear to school that day.

"See it right next to where the guys are standing." She froze like a statue. The response team bagged it and followed Dan and Helen into the shack between the jagged edges that the men had created. Helen rushed to keep up with Dan as he sprinted across the room. The men were gathered around a body.

It was a woman. Her blue sweater was soaked with blood. Her skin was the color of clear wax. "Roxanne. It's Roxanne. Was she stabbed?"

"Someone shot her," Dan said. "The coroner will take out the bullet and examine it."

Helen looked at the blood again. She hadn't remembered that much blood when the kidnapper was killed. Helen's stomach heaved. A sludge of chocolate backed up in her throat. "Dear God, Roxanne was killed in this shack. Amy was here. She could be dead. You've got to find her." Helen ran outside and threw up the bits of the U-no bar she had tasted at Kienow's.

When she climbed back into the shack, she held her head stiffly to avoid seeing the dead body. Dan met her at the entrance. "Was the deceased a friend of yours?"

"Deceased?" The word gave Helen the chills. "That's Roxanne. I told you about her when we talked about Erich's killer. She worked as a secretary in Administration and we ate lunch together sometimes."

"I know where she worked," Dan said impatiently. "What else do you know about her?"

Words came in a rush like throwing up. "What happened to her baby? She was pregnant with Erich's baby."

"Pregnant?" Dan repeated. "Did she tell you that?"

"She didn't have to. It was obvious. They were going to get married," Helen said, trying to balance everything that had happened. It made her dizzy.

"Jeez," Dan said, folding his hands the way he did when deep in thought. "Hey, Gordon, bag that strange pillow and bring it to me, please."

Gordon strolled over to them, holding a dull pillow, the size of needlepoint throw cushions her mother made. "What is that?"

"We found it on the body." Dan took the pillow from Gordon and held it out for Helen to see. "We weren't able to identify it until you informed me that she was pregnant, which she wasn't."

"Poor Roxanne. She was lying to us. She told us it was Erich's baby." Helen tried to look away, but she stood frozen, staring at the bloody blue sweater. Roxanne had loved that sweater. Though Roxanne's values were strange, especially about sex, and her brain was limited, Helen really liked her. Sometimes, she had even felt sorry for Roxanne.

She turned to Dan. "We need to find Amy."

His ears turned red. "We are working on that. This could all fit together." He put his arm around her shoulder and ushered her back to the rear of the hovel, where she suspected Amy had been.

The aura of death followed her. Men were spreading dark powder on the makeshift bedside table, the window frames, and the door.

"Why would Roxanne be involved with the kidnapping?" Helen asked. "She could be stupid at times, but never intentionally evil."

"We will know more after the lab work is completed. I'm not convinced that she was the kidnapper." Dan paused. "I know this is difficult for you. Could you check if anything in the room has changed since you were here?"

Helen scanned the room.

"We found something," an agent called.

Everyone from the other room rushed to join them.

Helen noticed the agent holding the same book she had seen earlier. "Amy, Amy?" Helen's shrill voice echoed off the walls. "*Goldilocks and the Three Bears*. That's how I knew she had been here."

"Bag it," Dan said, though the man had already opened a wax-paper bag.

Helen couldn't stop staring at the book. "That book will help you find the guilty person, won't it?"

"First we'll check any fingerprints other than Amy's with the prints on the shipyard files. If that doesn't work, we'll send them to the lab in Washington."

Helen listened as her impatience built. "What about the compact under the bed? I think it was Roxanne's."

"They've already bagged it, along with the items from the makeshift closet."

"It sounds like the procedure will take a long time. Amy is in danger and you need to do something fast."

Dan started to say something, then paused before he said, "As soon as the coroner finishes here, we'll work with our evidence at the Bureau."

She wondered what he had thought about saying but reconsidered. Maybe it was better not to have heard it. The two of them stood looking at each other without speaking.

Dan asked the evidence agent to bag some items in the living room. The two men walked away. Dan took a few steps back toward her. "You need to wait here until someone is free to take you home."

"I can drive myself."

"I'm sure you can, but it is out of the question."

Helen looked at the chipped paint on the walls, the holes in what were probably the dead kidnapper's blankets on the cot. "This room gives me the creeps."

"Come with me to the front room then."

"Roxanne's body is in there. I should drive home."

"Nothing is going to make me change my mind." He clasped her hand and led her back to the other area.

A motor coughed outside. Through the opening in the wall, Helen saw the coroner's truck park. Two men got out of the car, one carrying a medical bag and the other pushing a gurney, which he lifted to fit through the makeshift entrance.

Dan and the coroner placed Roxanne's lifeless body on the gurney and bent over her while the evidence agents examined the area on the floor where her body had been. Helen turned away from them.

After what seemed like hours, the gurney was rolled out with a white sheet covering Roxanne's body. That's all she was: a corpse hidden under a piece of cloth. Helen watched Roxanne disappear. It was so permanent. The thought of death made her feel faint. To get rid of this feeling Helen gazed around the room and focused on cigarette butts in an ashtray. One butt was a miniscule amount of cigarette with an extremely long extension of ashes. Someone must have left in a hurry, letting their cigarette burn out unattended. Helen watched as an evidence agent bagged the whole collection of burnt-out cigarettes and ashes. Her eyes moved to view the hotplate, which was crusted with layers of grease and crumbs. Poor Amy.

Helen turned to Dan. "Amy was in this *place*. She could be dead, too."

"That's not likely."

"Likely. I hate that word. It means nothing."

Dan looked at her. "Okay. From what we saw, the killer probably left in a hurry, leaving Roxanne's body behind." Dan stopped as though deep in thought. "He wouldn't have had time to hurt Amy."

Helen realized that he couldn't say "kill," though he also feared the worst.

Chapter Twenty-six

After all of the excitement at Sullivan's Gulch, Helen felt the absence of Amy the minute she walked inside her apartment. Dan would be busy for a considerable amount of time driving back to his office, studying the Coroner's report and checking the fingerprints. She had to get out of the apartment and walk off her frustration. The tech was reading a Batman comic book.

"Want to go for a walk?" Helen asked.

"I can't leave the phone," he said, barely looking up from the magazine.

Helen spoke in her most sincere voice, "I need the fresh air. I'll stick very close to home."

"I don't know." Tim paused, obviously conflicted. "Dan told me not to let you out of my sight."

"I'll be right out in front and I won't tell Dan that I had asked you to go with me."

He shrugged his shoulders. "Well, okay."

Helen ambled over to the schoolyard as she had done before Dan had put a curfew on her. It had become a ritual, which she saw as contact with Amy.

She almost stumbled over a dog. Was he dead? Helen bent down and touched him. He opened his eyes but didn't move. Poor thing. He was skinny, his fur dirty and tangled, and his neck was missing a collar. He was tiny, probably only a few months old. His eyes seemed to beseech her help. Maybe he was from a pet store. Someone could have bought him and, when taking care of him ceased to be fun, just thrown him out. The more she considered this dog, the more she wanted to care for him.

How could she take him to her apartment? She could carry him but dogs weren't allowed in the complex. As she walked away, the dog whined and tried to get up. His leg went out from under him. Poor thing. She picked him up. For the first time he wagged his tail and licked her face. Helen wondered if he had a name. What would someone who obviously didn't care about this dog name him? "Doggie?" He didn't react. "Puppy?" He wagged his tail. Maybe after she had the dog for a while she would try and change his name.

Amy would be so happy to have a dog, but Amy wasn't home. Helen swallowed the lump in her throat and concentrated on the dog. Soon they were in front of her apartment complex. She placed him under her blouse and shuffled into her apartment.

When she took him out of hiding, he cowered in her arms.

"Look what I found outside," she called to Tim.

He rushed into the living room. "A little pup. He looks neglected. How could anyone treat a dog like that?"

Helen was relieved to hear his concern. It signaled that he could be convinced to keep the dog. "I'm going to bathe him."

Tim scratched his stomach. "He's a cute little guy."

She carried the dog into the bathroom where she bathed him in the shower with Amy's baby shampoo. The sweet odor brought tears to her eyes. She leaned over the tile and cried. Puppy licked her face. Maybe she could keep him. She lifted him out of the shower. Water soaked her clothes. Amy would love him if she ever came home. *Don't say that; don't even think it.*

To blot out such thoughts, Helen wrapped Puppy in a towel and carried him to the kitchen. He sat and watched as she scrambled some eggs and put them in a bowl. With one bite, he swallowed the food then gulped water from the bowl where she had set it on the floor. The poor dog had been starved.

Helen noticed his rear leg was out of line. Tomorrow she would find a veterinarian. Puppy dragged his hind leg as he scooted over to Amy's chair and sniffed the seat. He grasped her teddy bear in his mouth and whined. Helen picked him up and took him into the bedroom where she placed him on the carpet. He thrust his snout upward and sniffed. She lifted him onto Amy's bed and he nestled under her pillow and barked. His barks turned into whining. Could it be? Thoughts electrified Helen's body. Could he be the dog that had wooed Amy? Stumbling over, she fell onto the bed next to Puppy and sunk into the thick quilt, overwhelmed by Amy's tiny, soft pillow.

Helen opened her eyes. A sliver of light shone through the blackout shades. She looked down to see Puppy cuddled in her arm. It was morning. Puppy licked her face. She had slept better than any other night since Amy had been missing. She got out of bed and brewed some coffee. Dan had not called. It became clear to Helen that she would have to continue investigating alone.

She returned to the bedroom and placed the dog on the floor and placed Amy's jacket beside him. He sniffed it and barked. He did the same to a sweater and a nightgown. She was increasingly convinced that this had to be the dog that had lured Amy.

In the kitchen, she poured herself a cup of coffee. While she drank it, she looked up veterinarians in the phone book and found one in Vanport. After she finished, she called the pet shelter and asked if anyone had reported a missing Cocker Spaniel.

"Lady, we get hundreds of calls. You have to come down here and see for yourself."

Helen hung up and redialed the number. "I'd like to report a missing dog."

"Hold on a second," a woman said in the same hostile voice of the previous conversation.

When another woman asked Helen if she could help her, she said,

"Has anyone reported a missing Cocker Spaniel? I found one and I'm wondering if someone lost him."

Without pausing the woman said, "I'm afraid not, but you're welcome to bring the dog down here."

"I will," Helen lied.

Puppy put his uninjured paw on her leg. She lifted him into her lap and dialed the veterinarian's number. She made an appointment for 9:30, which would give her an hour to dress and still get to the shipyard after the visit in time to test if Puppy would react to any workers. Helen put him down and scrambled all of her remaining eggs. That would be it until her next batch of ration stamps. She put some on a plate for herself and the rest in Puppy's bowl.

Helen took a few bites and shoveled her leftovers into the dog's bowl. She looked at the phone. Should she call Dan? No. She didn't want to talk about the dog or her planned visit to the shipyard. She slipped into her workshirt and coveralls. The bib would hold Puppy.

"How's he doing?" Tim asked as he strolled into the kitchen, startling Helen.

"I'm afraid he needs to see a vet. There's one close by." Helen was quick to add that before he could object.

"Gee, you're not supposed to leave."

"I'm sure no one would want to see the dog suffer."

"Promise me you will come right back," he said as a red flush moved up his neck.

Helen nodded. It wasn't really a lie because she didn't speak.

When they first got into the car, the dog whined. Helen put him on her lap and drove to the address she had for the vet adjacent to the shopping center. The building smelled of dog fur and urine, giving Helen doubts about the place. To divert her anxiety, she tried to think of names that would sound like Puppy so she could replace this innocuous name. *Guppy? Tuppy? Yuppy?* Helen liked Guppy.

Once she and Guppy were in the exam room, she noticed that the veterinarian was an older man, wearing a crisp white smock over khaki pants. His broad smile revealed large front teeth with wide spaces between them. He introduced himself as Dr. Gordon. Helen explained that this was a stray dog and she wanted to keep it.

He bent over Guppy. "This makes me so darn mad. People abuse dogs as if the poor pooches had no feelings." He listened to the dog's heart with a stethoscope, had the assistant take his temperature, and did a thorough exam. "This is one strong guy to have survived such treatment. He has been starved and beaten. I'm going to fluoroscope the leg."

He told Helen to wait in the reception room and left with the assistant carrying Guppy. Helen thought about the terrible odor. "Could I just wait here?"

"Make yourself comfortable," he called over his shoulder as he headed to a back room.

She paced back and forth until Guppy and the vet returned.

"The leg is only strained and not broken. I gave him a shot of pain medicine and wrapped the leg for support."

Helen was relieved and already thinking about her trip to the shipyard. "Can he walk or run?"

The doctor smiled. "Try and stop him. As soon as he is nourished, he will have more energy." He took a cookie from a jar and Guppy lapped it up. Helen picked Guppy up again and the doctor walked them to the door. "You can take the bandage off in a week."

She stopped at the variety store and wandered past Jaw Breakers, bubble gum, past douche bags and hot water bottles and down the aisle until she came to the dog section where she bought a collar, leash and some puppy chow.

When they returned to the car, he crawled into her lap again and stayed there all the way to the shipyard. Helen began to doubt her plan. She knew it was a long shot for the dog to recognize someone even though he had fussed over Amy's teddy bear and clothes.

Parking the car in a lot near the bus stop, Helen leashed the dog and walked close to the people getting off the buses. Guppy urinated in the bushes and sniffed the foliage. The pine scent overpowered most of the stink from the dog's waste. She kicked dirt to bury the mess and dragged Guppy closer to the workers. He continued walking at the same pace. Helen squared her shoulders to combat the feeling that her body would collapse. The dog had given her hope and taken it away at the same time.

Helen needed Guppy to fuss over someone who had kidnapped Amy. Maybe she had forced him to walk too soon. She thought about giving up, but she would have to wait for the FBI agents, who were slow as tortoises, to find Amy.

Suddenly the leash became taut and pulled Helen into a run. Her feet barely touched the ground. One foot tripped over the other and she extended her free arm to avoid falling. She yanked at the leash but Guppy kept running faster and faster, his nose sniffing the ground, causing Helen to lope along. First he had ignored the workers and now he raced toward them like a greyhound after a rabbit. Her spirits soared again at the thought that he might have sniffed a lead.

He moved from one lunch bucket to another. Helen felt like crying. She had been so sure he would lead her to the kidnapper, and all he wanted was food. Guppy shot forward again and stopped. She looked up to see Betty. Guppy sniffed Betty's leg and wagged his tail. Helen tried to catch her breath. Even though Guppy was sniffing Betty's lunchbox, Helen had already decided that Betty, herself, and not her food, had attracted Guppy because she was familiar to him.

Betty ignored him. "Well, look who's here. Sorry about your kid. They find her yet?"

Before Helen could answer, Guppy licked Betty's leg.

"Get away, you mutt." Betty kicked him. "I hate dogs."

"Well, he sure took a liking to you," Helen said as she picked Guppy up.

"That's the way it is. Dogs and cats always bother people who don't like them."

Helen wanted to ask her if she had ever seen Guppy before, but she was afraid Betty would be suspicious. She had to tell Dan what she had done, and that was all the trouble she could handle.

Charlotte ran over and hugged Helen. "Have you found your daughter yet?"

Helen shook her head. She inhaled Charlotte's lilac powder and remembered when her life was normal, when Amy went off to school with joy and Helen had a feeling of accomplishment and camaraderie at the shipyard.

"That is so sad, Charlotte said. "Keep your hope up. They'll find her."

Helen remembered how cheerful Charlotte had always been. Would she have said this if she were guilty? "I wish I had your optimism."

"What a darling dog," Charlotte said as she rubbed his neck.

He lay still and had no reaction. None at all, Helen noticed.

"Why don't you stay and have lunch with us, like old times," Charlotte said.

It wouldn't be like old times because Roxanne was dead. Helen decided not to tell Charlotte about her death because she didn't know if the news about the murder had come out yet. "I'd love to but I didn't bring any food and I'm afraid to leave my dog alone."

"That's okay, I'll share mine and we can sit outside."

"Count me out," Betty said. "I'm not eating with any damn dog." Guppy put his paw on her arm. "Stop it." She raised her arm to strike.

Helen grabbed him. "Don't you dare."

"Betty. You're such a coward," Charlotte said. "The dog is tiny and you're being mean."

When they reached the ships on the ways, Betty left without saying a word.

Helen considered telling Charlotte about finding Guppy, but Helen couldn't afford to trust anyone at that point. She simply said, "Betty never did like me."

"She treats everyone that way. Meet me at the administration building at noon."

Helen didn't mention that it would be convenient for her. No one needed to know she was going to snoop in Roxanne's desk again. She looked at the large clouds moving across the sky and hoped it wouldn't rain before she reached the building.

Chapter Twenty-seven

Helen headed for the administration center. Each time she saw the building she admired the grandness of the large span of white stucco and the row of tall windows. Helen stepped into the hallway. The astringent scent of cleaning fluid, the tap-tap of shoes, like a chorus of drums. She remembered how proud and happy she was when she had first signed up and received her identity badge. *I should never have come to work here*, she thought. This was no time for regrets. She was in the building for one purpose: to get evidence to find Amy.

She walked down a narrow hall to Roxanne's cubbyhole. Two men stood around Roxanne's maple desk. Helen recognized Dan. She wanted to turn and run, until she saw the framed posters on the plaster walls. A woman who looked like Heddie Lamar, next to a sinking boat, stared out over the words: WANTED FOR MURDER. "Her careless talk costs lives." The other poster showed Rosie the Riveter with her determined expression and the words: WE CAN DO IT, which reminded Helen why she had come to this building. The bunch of file folders in Dan's hand stirred her curiosity.

When Helen approached the men, the other agent gathered up the folders and left. There went her research. She smiled to hide her disappointment.

Dan smiled. "Helen, I was going to call you."

Helen recognized the troubled smile and knew that he had been informed of her absence from home and was probably furious that she had left her apartment. She returned his smile though she was unhappy, too. "I hope that means you have good news."

"What is that?" Dan asked, nodding at her coveralls.

Guppy had been sleeping, and Helen looked down to see his floppy ears hanging over the bib. "Why were you going to call me?"

Dan pointed at the ears. "Is that a dog in there?"

Helen didn't want to distract Dan from telling her about his latest inquiries. "You were saying you had news? I hope it's good."

"Let's go to my office and you can explain why you're carrying a dog around."

Helen looked down to see Guppy still sleeping. "I found this dog at the schoolyard and you should have seen him pounce on Amy's doll. He went nuts." She swallowed to avoid crying. "This is my evidence."

"Two ears?" Dan asked, clearly making fun of Helen. He led the way up some stairs to the security department and into a square room. It had the glue-like scent of new carpeting and was scantly furnished with a desk, filing cabinets, and two black Naugahyde chairs. The desktop was covered with tall piles of typed papers and a typewriter. An empty cup, with a dark ring of coffee stain inside, occupied the last available corner. He scooped up all but a few papers and shoved them into his briefcase. "Let's sit down and you can tell me about your evidence." He waited for Helen to sit in a chair before easing into his desk chair.

Helen thought she noticed a sarcastic tone in his voice, or was she being sensitive? She pulled Guppy from her bib onto her lap. Dan reached over to pet him. No reaction from the dog. Excitement flustered Helen. How should she present this? She put Guppy on the floor to try one more test. He ran around the room. He had lifted his leg before they came in, but she shuddered at the thought of him doing something on the new carpet. She concentrated on the fact that Guppy proved her point. "He's ignoring you."

"Dogs usually like me," Dan said in a tone expressing his disappointment.

"I could barely keep up with him when Betty walked by. He fussed over her. He ignored Charlotte. That led me to believe Betty was involved in the kidnapping."

Dan wrote on his notepad. "It would be perfectly normal for you to think every dog is the one used to lure Amy."

He was patronizing Helen. She struggled to control her anger. "I happen to think that this dog fits the profile."

Dan took a few pages from his briefcase and handed them to Helen. It was the file marked PERSONAL that she had seen in Roxanne's desk. The print had the smudged blue letters of a carbon copy. Each page had a list of ships that had been repaired.

"Roxanne was involved in the spy scheme?" Helen asked.

"She was obviously showing this information to someone."

"Who?" she asked.

"I don't know," he said.

Helen suspected that he did know and didn't want to tell her.

She said nothing for a few minutes while observing him. He stared at the carpeting rather than look at her, an action that proved her suspicion. Helen continued. "Here's what I think. Roxanne's body was found where Amy had been held." With the thought of Amy being in that hovel, Helen's body chilled. "Now with the evidence that Roxanne was leaking confidential information, it appears that the kidnapping and the spy operation are connected." Helen noticed Dan was twirling his fountain pen between his fingers, an act that annoyed her. The rest of her words rushed out. "But you knew that all along, didn't you?"

Dan looked at Helen, his face expressing something that was difficult to read. "What I do know is that you have been running around like a child as though the possibility that the deceased kidnapper had an accomplice did not exist."

What did he expect her to do? There was work to be done. "I am not a child and I have been more responsible than your whole FBI. I'm stronger than you think and I can't sit idle while my baby is in trouble." Her eyes felt swollen, but she was not going to cry.

"Okay, this is what we will do," Dan said in a positive voice. "You can work with me, just not alone."

"Not alone?"

"Absolutely not alone. I, or some agent, will be with you at all times. Tim has been replaced by a more experienced technician."

"That doesn't sound like working together. To me it feels like imprisonment."

Dan chose to ignore her remark. He handed her another page from Roxanne's folder. "You should feel honored. Most people don't get this privilege. By working together, I mean we will discuss aspects of the case." He pointed to the paper. "What do you make of this?"

Helen grasped the page and squinted at the smudged print.

You d n't appreciate me. It's time f r an answer.
If you don't ivorce her, I'm goi g to tell the police
you spied f r the J ps

"The carbon is smeared but it looks like a threat."

"It's one more carbon copy," Dan said.

Helen rubbed her fingers on the chair arms to calm herself. She considered Dan's dismissive remark his way of playing down the evidence. He really didn't want her to be involved. He had treated her like everyone else had, which she considered insulting. "You're just humoring me."

"What do you mean?"

"Like you don't know. If we are going to work together, you can't brush me off like you did about the carbon."

Dan frowned. "I just meant that we have a lot of evidence that needs evaluating."

Helen refused to let him get away with such a trite reply. "Such as?"

"Who killed Roxanne?" Dan rolled a pencil in his fingers. "Heck, we haven't even figured out who killed Erich, except it was someone he had attacked. We will discuss all of this."

Helen stood up. "I want to investigate with you, also."

"That's possible."

She looked at her watch. She would have loved to argue with him but there was no time. "I am supposed to have lunch with Charlotte. I can't cancel now."

Dan said, "I'll keep an eye on both of you."

She should never have mentioned meeting Charlotte. Helen would be humiliated if she spotted Dan spying on them.

Helen hadn't realized how much Dan's office had stifled her until she stepped outside and took in the limitless rows of buildings and ships. Charlotte was waiting on the front steps. Her peach complexion was as lovely as ever, and it was refreshing to be outdoors after the rain had stopped. The two women spread newspapers on the damp concrete and sprawled out at the edge of the steps. Helen thought about how Charlotte's ballerina walk had originally made her suspicious, and how she had seen Roxanne copy it so precisely. She decided not to mention Roxanne until Charlotte indicated her opinion of the kidnap.

Charlotte took out a package of Old Gold cigarettes and offered Helen one.

"I didn't bring my own, but I shouldn't take any from your limited allowance of cigarettes."

Charlotte handed Helen a cigarette. "You have enough on your mind."

Helen had never enjoyed smoking but recently she needed the diversion. She remembered Marcia's car where she and Joanne prepared Helen for college by teaching her how to smoke. A deep fog of smoke filled the car, casting the unpleasant scent of burnt tobacco. But Helen had continued towards her goal. She imitated them precisely and followed their instructions yet she was the only one who coughed and choked.

This reaction plagued her at Stanford when she tried to keep up with the other co-eds. Soon she gave up smoking.

Smoke rings filled the air as Charlotte puffed her cigarette and exhaled.

"Did you hear about Roxanne? It was on the radio this morning."

Helen looked around the wide porch and at the steps below. She was relieved that no one could hear their conversation and that Charlotte had already heard about the death. "First Erich and then Roxanne. Who would kill them?"

"She was playing with some questionable people." Charlotte stepped on her cigarette to put it out. She opened her lunchbox and took out a sandwich wrapped in waxed paper and put one half on a napkin for Helen.

Helen snuffed out her cigarette behind herself, not wanting Charlotte to see how little she had smoked, and concentrated on unwrapping the egg sandwich. When she looked up, she saw Dan across the street, leaning on a fire hydrant. Her skin itched with the feeling of being smothered. Helen forced herself to concentrate on Charlotte. She tried to compose a question without appearing overly curious. She was afraid to bring up the spy issue and hoped Charlotte would. "I still don't understand why Roxanne was murdered. She and Erich were lovers, which probably means he was also playing with questionable people."

"I don't know," Charlotte said quickly. "Let's eat our fruit on the way back to the ship."

"I'm sorry I was late," Helen apologized without revealing the reason for her having been stuck inside the building.

"Don't be. I should apologize to you. I am just so nervous about all the terrible things happening here and now I have to go to Tulle Lake again," Charlotte said as she pulled an apple and orange out of her lunchbox.

"Again?"

"It's a mess. My husband is in the Army and my mother-in-law is ill. I have written the Marshal to release my girl and boy, but I don't have anyone to take care of them and they won't be safe in public."

"What about your family?"

Charlotte shrugged. "They disowned me when I married a Japanese man." Charlotte looked at the fruit in her hands as though seeing it for the first time. "We can eat these as we walk. Which one do you want?"

"I am so sorry." Helen looked at the fruit. "You decide." She said quickly, not wanting to waste time until she got more information, though she didn't know how to turn the conversation back to the spy issue. For once she was glad to know that at least Dan was somewhere in the area. "I still don't understand why Roxanne was murdered."

Charlotte handed Helen an apple and started peeling the orange. "Me neither. Maybe it was lover's rage. I know she was seeing a man."

"Other than Erich?"

"This was a new romance. She told me about it last week."

"Darn. I missed that. I should have returned to work sooner."

Charlotte clasped Helen's hand. "You are brave to come back at all."

Helen hoped her hand wasn't shaking as much as she felt it had.

"She bragged about how well her new boyfriend treated her. I got the impression he was rich."

Helen saw workers walking toward the ships or plating shops, still carrying their lunch buckets. This reminded her that she had little time to get more information. "Anyone would be nicer than Erich. I'm sure you know that from your dealings with him."

"It's his wife I have to deal with," Charlotte said in a confessional rush as though she couldn't wait to speak. "Yesterday she refused to pay what they still owe me for the doll shop even though I went there and begged." Charlotte must have seen Helen in her car outside the shop and needed to explain why she was there. Did that mean Charlotte was more involved than she would admit?

"Can't you take action against her?" Helen asked.

"Japanese-owned property is worth nothing, and the store was in my husband's name."

"I'm so sorry," Helen said. Every time she spoke with Charlotte to clarify evidence she found more reasons to doubt her innocence, but still couldn't believe that this poor courageous person could hurt anyone.

"I'm used to it by now, but I could sure use the money."

Helen worried that Charlotte needed money. The need could have influenced her actions.

On the way home, Helen thought about how Charlotte appeared to be rushed after she told Helen about Roxanne's romance. Charlotte's short, almost dismissive answers troubled Helen when she tried to make sense out of their conversation. She would not talk about this to Dan. In fact, she was suffocating from his intrusion on her privacy and unable to utter a word. But maybe she should get Dan's input. He had experience, and this might be important. No, she couldn't give him the satisfaction.

As his car pulled up in front of her apartment, her need to get Dan's professional opinion won out. "Charlotte told me Roxanne had a new boyfriend and she was mixed up with questionable people."

"How do you know that Charlotte is reliable?"

"You have a point. I think she is a spy."

"What makes you think so, Sherlock?"

Helen didn't have time to be offended. "I saw her come out of the doll shop."

Dan turned his key in the ignition and revved the motor. "The doll shop? Now you have really put yourself in danger."

Chapter Twenty-eight

After Dan left, the technician made adjustments on the phone line, the squeaks and scraping noises worse than a fingernail scraping a blackboard. Helen couldn't stand it. She ran into her bedroom and threw herself on the bed. Rosie the Riveter looked out at Helen from the magazine on her bed table. Helen knew that Rosie would tell her to get out there and find Amy.

"I'll be right back," Helen called to the technician as she opened the door.

He raced over to her and blocked the doorway. "You are not allowed to leave alone."

Helen smiled. "Right back means in a few minutes."

"I have instructions. If this is important I can call for someone to drive you."

"You are all *driving* me nuts," Helen said, prancing into her bedroom where she locked the door and retrieved her backup car keys.

Thanks to her years at summer camp, she did an admirable job of plumping up her blanket to resemble someone asleep. Then she opened and closed drawers, noisily. While slamming a drawer with one hand, she opened the window with the other and slid out to her freedom. There were some advantages to living in a small, poorly built building.

Next, she had to deal with her mother, get into her basement and find a disguise that would fool the surveillance guys in front of Betty's place. Luckily, traffic was light and the bridge was not drawn up and there were no traffic cops on the way. The drive from Vanport to her parents' house took her twenty minutes. As Helen scooted up the front steps, she grasped their house key that she still had, and hoped her mother wasn't home. Just in case, she rang the bell and unlocked the door simultaneously. Her mother stood in the hall, holding splayed cards in her mauve-tipped fingers.

"I'm sorry to interrupt your bridge game."

"Not at all," her mother said. "Come say hello to the girls."

"I just came by to get some of my things from the basement," Helen said as she waved at the three women sitting at a card table in the living room. They looked like paper-doll cutouts with their curled hair and the large shoulder pads of their linen dresses.

Her mother frowned with her eyes half-closed, expressing sadness. "All of the past is in that one storeroom." She pulled Helen away from the living room into the hall. "Oh, Honey, you must come home and stay with us. When Amy comes back, we can be a family again."

"I need to stay near the shipyard and find out who took Amy."

Her mother's voice was sharp as a flute. "The FBI is better able than you to accomplish that. You should get out of that dangerous place. I couldn't bear it if something happened to you, too."

"Martha," a voice carried from the living room. "It's your deal."

Helen hugged her mother and whispered in her ear. "I love you and Dad very much but I am thirty years old and it's time for me to grow up." She gave her mother another hug and said, "You go ahead. I'll call you later."

"Be sure and take some of the peaches I canned."

On the way to the basement, Helen thought that if only she had been content to play bridge instead of doing war work, Amy would have been safe.

The light was dim and she carefully moved her feet from step to step until she reached the concrete floor. The area had the pungent smell of raw sawdust, left over from the furnace fuel before her parents converted to oil heat. The Halloween costumes were on shelves in a small storage closet above the jars of pickled cucumber and canned peaches. Helen pulled the box down and rustled through ballet tutus, clown masks and fake jewelry. No wigs. In another box, she found a Ouija board and was tempted to ask it if Amy was safe. Her hands shook so she moved on and managed to dig out her roller skates from under a catcher's mitt.

In the next box, Helen found a black wig along with black witch's clothes. The wig was enough. As an afterthought, she grabbed a jar of peaches so she could tell the truth when her mother would ask if she had taken any.

On her way back to the stairs, Helen saw the laundry chute and remembered how she and her friends played that ghosts were sliding into the basement. At this moment she didn't see it as fun. The partially lighted basement, the memories of ghost games, and the creaking steps as Helen climbed back upstairs caused her to visualize Amy. Did they keep her in a basement? Did they shut her in a closet? After getting the disguise, she ran up two sets of stairs and grabbed her old reversible raincoat from her closet. She hadn't worn it since her college days and was happy that her mother hadn't given it away.

Betty lived near downtown so Helen drove to the bus station on 5th and Taylor across from the parking lot where the workers would get off the bus.

While she waited she noticed the changes in Portland. Growing up she thought the city was boring. Not anymore. Where once just a few shiny cars cruised slowly along the streets, now a parade of cars sped by, in spite of gas rationing. Most pedestrian men wore Army or Navy uniforms, their creased pants, ties and perfect posture providing the only similarity to the adherence to proper behavior and dress in Portland before the war. The few women in Adele Simpson dresses and meticulously curled hair, which were once the norm, stood out among the throng of women in work clothes or slacks and T-shirts. They all, thin and fat, young and old had probably come to Oregon to work in defense plants. Though Helen worked beside such women in the shipyard, it felt strange to see them downtown.

The first shipyard bus pulled up to the curb and workers spewed out. Helen was surprised to see Betty come off the first afternoon bus. She had left the shipyard earlier than usual. Helen watched her trudge across the street to the parking lot. Away from the shipyard, Betty appeared older and shabbier. She slid into the seat of an old car. It was the same car that had been parked at Sullivan's Gulch.

Helen got so excited she stepped on the brake rather than the clutch. By the time she restarted the engine, Betty's car had disappeared into traffic. *Stupid,* Helen thought. She should have left the detecting to Dan and his agents.

Heavy rain punished the windshield. To the rhythm of the wipers, Helen held a conversation with Rosie. *Now that you are here, do whatever it takes to find Amy,* Rosie advised her. With her eye on the rearview mirror for police, she sped along Taylor Street in the direction she had last seen Betty's car, dodged oncoming traffic to pass several cars, and eased back into the lane to follow the Studebaker behind Betty's car. Betty turned onto 3rd Street while the Studebaker continued forward.

Helen slowed down until another car passed her and followed the two cars until Betty's car pulled up to the curb in front of an old wooden house with a hammock on the front porch. Helen jotted the address on a piece of paper and drove around the block to park at the corner across the street where she could still see Betty's house.

Helen's skin itched as she waited and watched the house. Betty would eventually need to drive somewhere. Helen hoped that didn't mean the next morning. The rain had let up, but to be safe, Helen turned her reversible coat to the rain side and put a scarf in the pocket. Then she waited some more. Her neck ached. Would she be able to out-wait Betty? Helen thought about going home for the night and returning after Betty was at work. No. She couldn't take a chance. The bobby socks, which were part of her disguise, had left her legs bare. They felt like two icicles.

It took another hour for Betty to come out to her car. Helen waited until Betty had driven away before she scooted her feet into the roller skates, tightened the toe clasps with a key to fit her saddle shoes, and buckled the straps. Then she put on the black wig and shoved her hair under it. At first, the skating made Helen shaky and she extended her arms for balance. But soon she was skating like a teenager up the side street.

Betty's house was second from the corner and backed up to a dead-end street. Helen skated onto the road until she reached the house. She took off her skates, tied the straps together and slung them over her shoulder.

At the top of the tiny back porch, Helen tried the door, which was locked. She concentrated on the closest window. She had to cut the screen with her Varga Girl pocketknife. Once cut, the screen yielded easily. The window was opened a small crack. Helen scraped her knuckles when she shoved her fingers under the sash, but it was worth the pain. She was able to gain enough space to crawl into the kitchen. Orange peels and dirty dishes floated in murky water in the sink. Helen wondered if this was the house that Betty had talked about buying with their salaries from the shipyard. Helen felt the presence of Betty and her dead husband. Her shoulders shivered. She moved into the living room, where dust mites floated over the sofa and filled the room with a musty used-book odor. She looked for signs of Amy. An ashtray full of ashes and the stink of stale tobacco repelled Helen but gave her no clues. She had to move on.

In the entry hall, the banister by the narrow steps had been worn down to its bare wood. She scooted up the stairs to the second floor and looked out a window. Betty's car was not there yet. Helen knew she had to make good use of the limited time until Betty would return. She stared at two closed doors before opening the first one. Every inch of space was covered with clothes, boxes and fishing rods. She looked carefully at the mess but could find nothing that had belonged to Amy. No small clothes and not even a book.

The next room must have been an ordinary bedroom that had never been cleaned or painted. The closet was full of clothes. Helen pushed them aside quickly. She couldn't admit that she was looking for Amy's body. A deeply scarred cherry wood dresser stood beside the closet. Helen knew time was limited. She opened the top drawer and ruffled through some sweaters. On the bottom she saw a gun and slammed the drawer shut. She thought about the puddle of blood under Roxanne. The sight of a gun and the memory of Roxanne's body compelled Helen to leave immediately. She ran out into the hall.

Through the window, she saw Betty's car in the driveway. She raced to the stairway. From behind she felt a large, heavy body bumping into her, and muscular arms grasping her waist. Betty's cheap gardenia perfume was a backdrop for the situation. Helen reached for the banister but Betty tightened her grip. Helen couldn't breathe. She looked at the hall below and imagined her head hitting the wood floor. Betty was going to throw her down. The fall would kill her. Helen took a deep breath and looked straight ahead. Air caught in her tight chest. Sweat ran from under her arms and soaked her T-shirt. She had to do something, but what?

She moved her arm slowly and let it spring backward to pull Betty's hair. She missed. Betty grabbed Helen's wrist and twisted it. Pain sent electric-like shock up and down her arm. That was stupid, she told herself.

"I just wanted to find my daughter. You must understand how frantic I am."

"Well, I ain't got her and you put me in a pickle. Now, I can't let you go."

Helen didn't know what to do. Betty's grip around her waist was so strong she couldn't move. What would Rosie do? Certainly, she wouldn't give up.

"Step down, or I'll push you," Betty said, her voice agitated.

Helen stared at the steps. She would never survive the fall onto the hardwood floor below, but Betty had her locked in. Helen bent her waist, which made Betty's grip tighter. Helen could hardly breathe. Her waist burned. She bent a little farther until she was inches away from Betty's arm. Helen bit Betty as hard as she could. Her flesh tasted like rotten chicken, which, mixed with blood, caused Helen to retch. The taste of bile backed up in her throat.

"Ouch," Betty cried as her arm flew outward.

Helen pulled away, grasped the banister and slid down, landing in the hall. Heavy footsteps sounded behind her. Trying to ignore them, she opened the front door but Betty caught up with her on the porch and blocked the stairs. Helen's breath came in short gasps. She took in the scene: Betty's raised arm, her knuckles, and rain glistening on a knife blade. Helen grabbed her skates from her shoulder and aimed them at Betty's arm, but hit her face, bathing it in blood.

Helen couldn't stop to measure the damage.

The FBI agents who were running toward the property could go inside and call an ambulance. One of them, a guy with blond fuzz on his chin, stopped her. Before he could say anything, Helen spoke: "She's your kidnapper." Even though she hadn't proven this yet, she just knew it was true.

"Who are you?" the kid asked.

Helen pulled off the wig that had let her bypass them to get into the house. "The mother of her victim."

"You better come with me." He grasped her arm.

"I was just searching for my child. That woman tried to kill me."

"You can explain that when we get to the Bureau."

Chapter Twenty-nine

After Dan had left Helen at home, he went back to his office and read the lab report about Roxanne. Her fingerprints revealed that she had no criminal record. But she was dead and her prints on Amy's book would do him no good.

Dan looked up to see an agent lead a lady into his room. "I found this woman breaking into the house that we had been watching."

He nodded for the guard to leave and observed the young girl, scanning her from her saddle shoes up to her bobby socks to her over-sized raincoat and messy hair. It was Helen, not the Helen he knew, but definitely her. What in hell was she doing there? "Are you nuts? When are you going to learn that these dumb things you are doing are dangerous and not going to solve the case?"

"I found a gun there," Helen said timidly.

"What the devil did you do with it?"

Helen slid down in her chair, the friction of her body squeaking the Naugahyde.

Dan moved some papers around his desk to calm down. He remembered when Helen had first come to his office where she sat in the same chair on the other side of his desk. That was the day he took her out to lunch and that was the day he fell in love with her. Deny it as much as he wanted, but the rush of craving returned every time he saw her. But the depth of these feelings aside, he was still embarrassed that he had let his worry over her interfere with his duty. He lowered his voice. "Do you have the gun with you?"

Helen gave him a quizzical look. "I left it in the top drawer of the dresser and I didn't touch it."

Dan sighed with relief. "Good." He answered his phone, listened and hung up. "Sit there for a minute and don't move." What was he going to do now? He was needed down in the jail and didn't dare leave Helen alone. He dialed the main office. "Send a rookie up here immediately, preferably Gerson."

Helen stood up. "I'm going home now."

"Not so fast," Dan said. "I am having an agent drive you home and stay with you until I am free."

"That's ridiculous."

Dan laughed, mainly because she made him nervous. He also admired her spunk. "I should put you in jail for breaking and entering."

Helen didn't react. She probably knew as well as he did that this would not happen. When the rookie knocked on the door, Dan met him in the hall and gave him instructions on how to deal with Helen.

As she and the rookie left, Helen looked back and gave Dan a withering look. He felt immediate cramps in his abdomen. His attention shifted as he raced down the stairs to the basement jail. His training had taught him to compartmentalize, though that was before he had met Helen.

He took a minute to compose himself before looking at the large woman with bandages on her face and arm.

She paced back and forth in the small cell. "It's about time."

Dan recognized her as Johnson's widow. This excited him but he wasn't sure how soon he could shift to the kidnapping from the use of a knife. He backed away from the cell and asked the deputy if he had any forms from the surveillance.

"They asked me to inform you," he said, obviously embarrassed. "It's kind of delicate. They were watching the house in connection to a kidnapping and threatening someone with a knife is not their arena, especially when the victim broke into the widow's house."

Dan knew the officer was capable in dealing with arrests because they had worked together before. Even if this was sticky, Dan would have preferred more information and tried to hide his annoyance by being brief. "Bring the prisoner up to my office. I'll take care of this." On his way upstairs, Dan asked Albert to join him.

Albert sat in the extra chair at the end of Dan's desk while Betty sat across from Dan, her fat bulging at her waist. "So what should I'a done when I seen a robber in my house?"

"Where did you take the girl?"

Betty scratched the bandage on her wrist. "You're nuts."

Dan was silent and Albert followed his lead. They didn't have to wait long.

"My husband did it," she broke without further coaxing. "He and Roxanne," Betty said. "I had nothing to do with it."

"Where did you take the girl?" Dan repeated.

"Hey, I ain't talking unless there's a deal for me."

"We're your best chance," Dan said, hoping his face didn't show the lie. "If you level with us, I'll put in a good word for you with the federal prosecutor. You need us to get you a deal."

"Hey, I didn't do anything. Like I told ya, it was my husband and Roxanne."

Albert leaned forward in his chair. "You were involved in this with your husband. Tell me where the child is and it will go easier for you."

"Mike could see dollars anywhere. He said this was foolproof."

"We already know about him," Dan said. "You got the dog that lured the child." Dan decided he owed Helen an apology for not paying attention to her dog experience with Betty.

"That's all I did. Mike made me do it. He could be real mean."

One of the evidence agents knocked on the door and, without waiting for an answer, walked into the room and handed Dan an evidence bag. He spoke in a low voice. "Agent Miller, we found this gun that Mrs. Brooks saw in the Johnson house."

"Did you get fingerprints?"

"Yes, sir, your team will know the results today or tomorrow morning."

Dan took a deep breath and waited for the agent to leave, before turning his attention to Betty. "Tell us about the gun found in your house."

"My husband had a gun. Not me. I never used it."

Albert stood up. "Right now we are going to arrest you for attempted murder. Once the gun has been examined, we'll add other charges. This is your last chance to tell me where the girl is."

"This ain't fair. I don't know where she is. Roxanne moved somewhere with her. I want a lawyer."

Albert squeezed his lips into a forced smile. "Once you get a lawyer, you can kiss any deal goodbye."

Dan joined in: "You know how much sympathy kidnapped children get. A jury is going to give you the death penalty."

Betty slumped down in her chair. "Okay, okay, I'm gonna tell ya." She stopped and squeezed her lips shut, then open. "Roxanne wasn't ever pregnant. Erich made her have an abortion. The guy messed up and she couldn't have children." Betty leaned her head back and laughed. "The poor girl went nuts. All she wanted was a kid, she said. She'd a done anything to get one. I put her in touch with my husband, and he cooked up this scheme. He would get the money and she would keep the kid. That's all I did." She looked at Dan. "Yeah, and I found the dumb mutt in a pet store."

Dan was flushed. He had never realized his office was so small. It seemed as though Betty and Albert were crowding him against his desk. The wall with his framed diploma from the academy and watercolors of the capital in Salem crowded him. He loosened his collar button. "Kidnapping on federal property can get you the death penalty."

Albert shoved a tablet in front of Betty. "If you write all of what you told us it will help lessen your penalty."

"Right," Dan said quickly. "But first tell us where the child is." He was afraid Albert would accuse her of killing Roxanne and Betty would clam up.

"I don't know. Roxanne took her away. She is hiding somewhere with the kid."

Dan drummed his fingers on the table. Betty couldn't be trusted but what she said was probable. She clearly didn't know that Roxanne was dead. Without her help, it would be almost impossible to locate where Roxanne had taken Amy. "You must have some idea where they would go."

"I got no idea."

"Why are you protecting Roxanne? She left you to take the blame."

"Cross my heart, I don't know."

Dan didn't believe her. Or maybe he just didn't want to consider the permutations of Amy being alone or taken away by someone else.

He called for the deputy to take Betty back to her cell. After they left, he stood up and leaned across his desk to shake Albert's hand. "You were great. The information you got will help us when we put all of it together." Dan was pleased and a little proud that it didn't bother him to credit Albert.

His pride meant nothing as he realized the possibility of finding Amy had diminished.

Chapter Thirty

Amy liked the new house better than the other place, especially the flowered wallpaper. She was looking at the new book that the lady, who told her she was Diane, had bought. She liked the one about *Goldilocks and the Three Bears* that they had left at the ugly house, better. This one, *Red Riding Hood*, was a little scary.

Diane came into the room and put Amy on her lap. Amy didn't like to be there but she was afraid to move. The smell of Diane's perfume made Amy's nose itch.

"Want me to read you a story?" Diane asked, already opening the book.

"Okie dokie," Amy said, using the words her friends at school had taught her.

"You can call me Mommy."

"I already have a mommy." Amy tried to be brave and not cry.

Diane pinched her arm. "Soon there will three of us and then you will call me Mommy."

Amy rubbed her arm where Diane had pinched it. Three, Amy thought. She could count and she and Diane were two. Amy didn't want that bad man to be her father. "I already have a mommy and daddy."

The phone rang. Diane opened the door and ran out. Amy stood in the doorway and listened.

"Hi, Big Guy. You coming over now?"

It was quiet.

"You said we'd be a family."

Amy waited impatiently.

"Yeah, well I don't want the kid anymore. I'm going to do something you won't like."

Diane was quiet and Amy waited to hear more.

"Okay, I won't, but you have to promise me we'll all be together."

"All" means a lot of people. Amy was afraid that Diane meant her, too. She had to get out of there. She listened to hear where Diane was. There was no sound. Then her voice got louder as she said, "I'll get the damn money if you promise to take me someplace nice tonight."

Amy closed the door and ran back to the bed.

Diane opened the door. Her eyes were red like Mommy's when Daddy yelled at her.

"I have to go out for a little while," she said. "You stay right here. If you leave, I'll find you and hurt you really bad."

Amy hid her hand under the covers and crossed her fingers. "I won't. I promise." Amy watched Diane close the door and heard the lock click on the outside. She waited until her footsteps silenced and the car quit coughing. She looked out the window. The awful car was gone. She changed into the clothes she had worn when the man took her. They still smelled like Mommy's lotion and they didn't itch like the stuff Diane had bought her.

Amy tried to turn the doorknob but it wouldn't move. She ran over to the window and stood on her tiptoes to unlock it. The lock stuck. She reached both hands and tried again. She sat down on the floor and cried. *Don't be a baby.* She remembered looking at Flash Gordon in the Funnies. She would do what she had seen him do when he was in trouble.

She dragged the lamp over to the door, lifted it with both hands. It was so heavy she almost fell down but she stood still just like in the Funnies and swung it against the door as hard as she could. The wood crunched like torn paper and a piece fell to the floor. She reached her hand through the hole. It scraped her skin. She was brave. Walking with her fingers she found the lock and turned it. Pop went the lock. She opened the door and ran outside.

The minute Amy stepped outside she started to shake. Where should she go? Not the neighbors' houses. She was afraid of anyone near this place. Amy looked at the sky. Dark clouds moved but sunlight peeked between them. She looked at her Orphan Annie watch. Mommy had taught her how to tell time. The small hand was at two and the large hand was at six. Two-thirty. It would be light for a long time. She reached into her skirt pocket and found a dime. She could go to a movie but she wanted to go to her real home. Maybe if she kept walking she could find a bus that would go where Mommy worked.

Every time a car passed by the empty sidewalk, Amy walked faster. She passed tiny houses like the one she had left and had no idea where she was going. Tired and hungry, she kept walking until she saw buildings with lots of windows, like Roos Brothers in Palo Alto where Daddy bought his shirts. She knew these were not houses. She must have been closer to downtown. In front of one of the buildings, she saw men in undershirts with hair poking out like a porcupine, their shoulders bent over. One of these awful men stood up and walked funny behind Amy. "Damn Japs, damn war." She could hear his shoes on the sidewalk go from one side to the other.

He was so close Amy could smell the same kind of drink that Daddy drank during the cocktail hour. Tears ran down her face. She wanted to turn and run back to the yucky house, but she was not a scaredy-cat. By now, she could hear two men following her. What should she do? She ran and didn't look back. When it was really quiet, Amy slowed down. She saw a bus stop a few blocks away and kept walking. The closer she came, the farther she seemed to be from the bus.

Cars sounded like a stuck record on the phonograph. One car slowed down and drove alongside her. She had learned her lesson. She would not go with anyone again, even if they had a dog or promised her anything. Her heart jumped as she walked straight ahead.

"Amy." The voice came from the car. It sounded like Daddy but she wasn't sure so she didn't stop.

"Amy, Honey. It's Daddy." She turned and recognized her dad's car. He smiled at her through his open window. "C'mon, I'll give you a ride."

"Daddy." Amy climbed into the car. "I could have found my way," she said to show she was brave.

"That's okay, Pumpkin, I'll take you home now."

"Goodie." Amy couldn't wait. They were going to all be together. She longed to see Mommy and sleep in her own bed and play with her toys. "Can you have dinner and stay with us?"

"First we have to let the police know that you are okay."

Amy noticed that Daddy sounded worried. "Are we picking up Mommy?"

"She will be there." Daddy smiled.

"I want to see Mommy first."

"We have to report that you've been found."

Amy cried. "I want Mommy now. I'm hungry."

Daddy turned the car into a parking lot and pointed at a building. "Look at that funny clock on the building. That is Tip Top Drive-In." He parked the car in front of the restaurant. "We can get a milkshake and when we are through eating, then we'll see Mommy. Will you be good at the police station if we do that?"

Amy was really hungry, but she didn't want to wait to see her mommy. A lady in white pants and a red, white and blue top came to the window. Amy knew that those were the colors of the flag like the one in school.

Daddy ordered a vanilla milkshake and coffee.

"How will she know where we are?" Amy felt like she was going to cry.

"Mommies know those things."

The lady brought their drinks. Amy sipped her milkshake. It tasted yummy. "Is Mommy there yet?"

Daddy laughed. "Not yet." He sipped his coffee.

Amy watched the steam come out of his cup. "Let's go."

"Finish your milkshake. Mommy won't be there yet."

Amy sipped her milkshake. That was the only way she could go see her mommy.

Daddy smiled. "Pumpkin, you know your mom and I are not together anymore."

Amy put her milkshake back on the tray and placed her hands over her ears. "No. Don't say that."

Her daddy drank some coffee. He said, "One of these days, I might find someone to marry and she would be your stepmom."

She got her milkshake back and sipped the cold ice cream through her straw. It made her nose shiver, but she kept sipping her drink. She didn't understand what he meant. Step means stair or sometimes her mommy told her to step faster. And one of the girls at school had said, "Step on a crack and break your back," when they played hopscotch.

"Maybe you can live with me and your new stepmom," Daddy said after he had paid the lady.

Now she got it. Mom. A different mommy. *Step, step, step.* Amy hated the word. She would never say it again. She would never play hopscotch with that girl again. She closed her eyes until the car stopped, and she opened them to see a large building with clay dolls near the roof.

Chapter Thirty-one

Dan sat at his desk, sipping coffee from his mug. It was cold and bitter. His phone rang and the receptionist told him there was a problem up front. What more could go wrong?

Dan approached the receptionist. She nodded at a small child standing nearby. Dan noticed the child's red hair and realized it was Amy. How did she get there? He looked into her pleading green eyes.

"Can you call Mommy? I want her to come get me."

"You bet I will." Dan said, trying to keep his voice from shaking, so that he wouldn't scare the child. He used the phone on the mahogany desk and called Helen. "Amy is here at the Bureau."

He barely got the words out before Helen started speaking non-stop. "Are you sure it's Amy? She must be scared. Is she all right? How did she get there? I'll be right there."

Dan wished that he could just leave and celebrate with her. "Your mommy will be here soon, Amy," he said, savoring the moment. In his work, he was seldom the giver of good news.

Amy rewarded him with a hug around his waist. She stepped back and looked up at him with a huge smile.

Edgar stepped between the two of them, his wingtip shoes spread apart, his hands splayed on his hips. "I've come to tell you that I found my daughter wandering the streets."

He bent down to look at Amy. "Tell the man how nice I am to you."

Dan knew it was going to be difficult to stay objective with this man. "How did you know where she was?"

"I didn't know. I was just driving back to my hotel when I saw her all alone. At least I found her when you couldn't."

Dan felt pressure on his jacket and looked down to see Amy's green eyes staring at him. "I was running away from that crazy lady."

It was a good thing she had interrupted him because he was about to act extremely unprofessional. "I know you did, Honey. That was a very brave thing to do. I want to hear all about it in just a few minutes."

Amy walked away and sat in the chair closest to the door, obviously to wait for Helen.

Dan asked the receptionist to keep an eye on Amy and turned back to Edgar. "Let's go to my office." On the way, he looked through Albert's open door and beckoned Albert to follow.

Sitting around his desk in the crowded room, the three men looked at each other.

"I found my daughter, Amy, wandering alone down town," Edgar blurted before Dan could say anything.

Albert looked from Edgar to Dan. "That's interesting."

Edgar's face flushed. "I don't understand you men. I find Amy while you are spinning your wheels. I would expect some appreciation.

Dan became alert. At that moment, this was not Helen's husband. It was a criminal and Dan was going to nail him. "Maybe if you would explain how you knew where to find Amy, we might admire you."

"I was driving back to my hotel and there she was alone, walking on the sidewalk."

Electricity whizzed through Dan's chest. He knew a lie when he heard one and this one was obvious. "Someone tip you off about her?"

"Of course not. With Amy missing, I was alert to any small child walking alone."

Dan struggled to control his anger. "We assume that Amy had been found walking not far from the place where she had been held. On the other hand, you could have chosen any of a dozen streets to drive through town."

Edgar straightened his shoulders and leaned forward. "Do I need a lawyer?"

"We could wind this up fast," Albert said. "If you had no part in the kidnapping, you'll be free to go."

"Kidnap my own daughter? You're in cahoots with your partner." Edgar looked as though he were going to spit on Dan. "He wants me out of the picture."

Albert shot back, "Being such an attractive woman, Roxanne could have talked you into anything."

"You guys are desperate. I want a lawyer."

Dan was about to embellish on what Albert had said, when his phone rang. *Saved by the bell*, he thought.

 Dan answered his phone to hear the receptionist tell him that Helen had arrived. Albert stood up. "We'll be right back." Dan followed Albert out and spoke rapidly. "I've been called to reception," Dan said, not mentioning Helen. "Let's face it. With Roxanne dead, we can't prove he was in on the kidnapping." He hated to admit this when deep down he knew that Edgar was guilty. He had to be honest with himself. If it had been just another suspect and not Helen's husband, it would have been easier to let go. This wasn't the first time a witness had been killed. Somehow he would get the guy.

Albert seemed relieved. "My thoughts exactly. I'll start the release."

Dan didn't have time to consider Albert, but it appeared that the two of them had just agreed on something.

He spotted Helen and Amy as soon as he entered the reception room. They were hugging each other. It was the first time he had seen Helen smile, her whole body bent contentedly. He strode over and put his arms around the two of them, then stood back and observed mother and daughter with their red hair and green eyes and the way they became one with their embrace.

"Are you and Mommy friends?" Amy scrunched her face into a

frown. "You can't be my stepdaddy."

Dan could feel his face burn. It was probably bright red. "Where did you hear that word?"

"Daddy told me one day I would have a stepmommy and I would live with the two of them."

"Let's go to a nice room and you can tell me about it." Dan led them to a conference room. Being in his small office with Helen would distract him.

Amy climbed up into one of the chairs. "And one of the ladies told me that I should call her Mommy and there would be three of us. I didn't like the mean man or the other woman."

"My God, " Helen said. "Edgar was up to his old tricks but this time with a criminal. He was…." Dan thought Helen had stopped because she was going to describe an inappropriate act. Amy's remark about a stepdaddy had embarrassed him enough. He forced himself back to the conversation with Amy. "So this woman took care of you?"

"Sometimes the mean man did."

"What did he look like?"

Amy laughed. "Charlie, umm…" She turned to her mother. "Who, Mommy?"

"Charlie Chapman," Helen guessed. "Did the man have a mustache?"

Amy nodded her head. Dan looked at Helen. He guessed from her question that she suspected it was the man who had come for the ransom. It excited him to share an unspoken thought with Helen. He had to face it. She excited him, period.

Edgar burst into the room, followed by agents, who were about to handcuff him.

"For Christ's sake, we're in conference here." Dan was furious. He felt as though Edgar had interrupted his intimacy with Helen. *Get a grip,* he said to himself. He barely knew her.

"I would like to know what is going on," Edgar said as though he were in charge rather than a suspect. "I save my daughter and, rather than getting custody, I am treated like a criminal." He looked at Amy.

"Tell them, Pumpkin, how I saved you and the fun we had at the drive-in."

"The milkshake froze my nose," Amy said. "And I wanted to see Mommy."

"Custody?" Repeating the word made Helen feel she was going to explode. "If you ever mention that word again, I'll see that you go to jail." She paused until the buzzing in her head stopped. "The first thing I am going to do is demand that you pay the back child support."

Edgar turned to Dan as though he would attack him. "How can you let her talk like that?"

"She's the one who can press charges," Dan said. "We suspect you were complicit in the kidnapping. The fact that you didn't call the authorities when you first knew the woman had your daughter makes you guilty of abetting a crime. Helen can claim you had intent to harm her child."

"Our child. Did you hear me?"

"Not anymore," Dan said, smiling.

"This is prejudice loud and clear," Edgar said.

Dan felt shame when he realized that he had enjoyed harassing Edgar. He promised himself that he would prove the jerk guilty.

Chapter Thirty-two

Helen blocked out the sight of Edgar and watched Dan. It was the first time he had smiled for a while. Amy was safe and Dan was competent. She wanted to lean over and kiss him.

"I'm not saying another word until I get a lawyer," Edgar said.

"Did Daddy do something bad?" Amy said.

I am a terrible mother, Helen thought. She had such resentment toward Edgar that she had forgotten Amy was listening. "He will be all right, Honey." She held Amy's hand and led her out of the room to the reception area.

"You know what scared me the most?" Amy said, once they were seated on a loveseat together.

Helen controlled the horror that had crowded in on her as she heard about Amy's dreadful experience. "No, what?"

"When the lady took me in a car and covered me with a blanket, even my face."

"You had a blanket over your face?" Helen tried to disguise her anxiety so as not to upset Amy. "That is scary, Honey. Why don't we try and guess what she didn't want you to see."

Amy laughed. "You go first."

That was the first time Amy seemed happy since her return and Helen wished they could stop the conversation right there. But she couldn't let Amy's kidnapper go unpunished. "She had a surprise for you?"

"She didn't like me anymore."

Helen put her arm around Amy. "I can't imagine anyone not liking you."

"When I uncovered my face, she made me put the blanket back or she'd hurt me."

"You were a brave girl and now you are home. " Helen said, trying to stifle her outrage by noting her relief when she thought about what could have been done to Amy.

"Maybe she didn't want me to see the other person."

"I bet you're right." Helen took a deep breath to control her interest. "Now let's guess who the other person was."

"It was someone with a heavy whisper. They sounded like you and Daddy when you think I'm asleep."

Helen could barely control herself. It was Edgar. How could he do such a thing?

Dan came into the room and bent down to speak to Amy. "How would you like to draw a picture with Marge over there?" He pointed at the reception desk.

Amy held Helen's hand so tightly it became numb. "No. I want to stay with Mommy."

Helen hugged Amy. "You can be with me all you want, Honey. This man is like a policeman and he won't let anyone hurt you."

"Do you have a knife?" Amy asked Dan.

"No, I don't. Knives are very dangerous."

"The mean man had a knife. He tried to hurt Diane once." Amy put her hand on Dan's arm as though testing him. "Can he find me?"

Dan smiled at her. "He's gone far away. We won't let him come back."

"Do you have a gun?"

"Yes, I do, but I keep it locked. Guns are bad like knives."

"The ugly mean lady had a gun."

"The lady you called Diane?"

"No, the ugly one. She called me a brat."

"She was so wrong. You are sweet and brave." Helen thought the conversation was too frightening for Amy. "We should go home now, Honey."

Amy squeezed her eyes as though she would cry. "I want us to stay with Dan. He can hurt bad people."

The men and women coming through the door floated in front of Helen as they came through the entrance door. "I have hot dogs for dinner, Honey."

"I hate hot dogs. Diane gave them to me all the time."

Dan smiled at Amy. "Would you two ladies like to go to dinner with me tonight?"

Helen kept staring at Amy. She couldn't get enough of seeing her. Amy was back. Energy pulsed through Helen's body. She wanted to dance, dance and shout that Amy was home. She was impressed by the way Dan paid attention to Amy, and Helen felt a new excitement around him, but she cautioned herself against moving too fast.

Amy sucked her thumb, which meant she was ready for sleep. Helen could only imagine how terrible the last few days had been for Amy. "I think I better get Amy home. She is falling asleep." Helen debated about asking him for dinner. He had invited them out. "Come over later. I'll scrounge up some dinner."

"I'll be there as soon as I can."

When Helen parked in front of their apartment building, Amy woke up. "Where is the nice man?"

"He'll be here later." Helen heard Guppy wining on the other side of the door. "I have a surprise for you inside."

As soon as they walked through the door, Amy saw Guppy and ran over to hug him. He licked her hand. She lay down and he crawled over her body and licked her face. She laughed. Helen took in the sounds. It was like music. She had been afraid she would never hear Amy's voice again.

"Can we keep him, Mommy? He's just like the dog the bad man had."

"He is your dog, Honey." Helen decided not to talk about how she found Guppy until Amy was over the trauma from being kidnapped. "Come help me feed him."

Helen let Amy pour the kibbles in a bowl while she fixed Amy a tuna fish sandwich and some fruit. After her dinner, Helen supervised Amy's shower and tucked her into bed with the dog.

Helen opened cans of string beans, cream of mushroom soup, tuna fish, and her mother's peaches. She poured some crème de menthe that she had brought from California over the peaches and put them in the icebox. She put the casserole of the canned goods in the oven. Helen checked on Amy and Guppy, who were sleeping.

Dan had brought a bottle of Bourbon and one of lemonade. While he mixed the whiskey sours, Helen asked him if he had learned any more about the spy ring.

"Charlotte is innocent," Dan said as he carried the drinks into the living area where they sat on the sofa. "Erich's widow had traveled to various hotels in the cities matching the addresses on envelopes returned from Buenos Aires. The printed letters matched the typewriters in the hotels. Her lawyer wouldn't let her confess. The Attorney General will nail her."

Helen was relieved. She was never fully convinced that Charlotte had committed a crime. "Who killed Erich?"

"It was self-defense," Dan said. "He tried to push Roxanne overboard. Our post-mortem exam of her showed that her fingernails matched the scratches on Erich's face."

"Who hit him with the wrench?" Helen asked. Now that Amy was safe Helen could concentrate on the other crimes.

"Roxanne did. It must have boomeranged because they found broken skin in the weapon's shape on the palm of her hand."

Helen remembered the letter she found that had been retrieved from Erich's locker and wondered if Charlotte were a suspect. "So the only two arrests are Betty and Edgar."

"Don't forget the widow," Dan said.

"That's three."

He smiled, obviously uncomfortable, and handed the glass to Helen. "We didn't have any evidence to refute Edgar's supposed coincidence and had to let him go."

Helen sipped her drink. This was better for Amy, which pleased Helen, though the image of Edgar harassing her was frightening. "I am happy Amy won't be plagued by having a criminal for a father."

The doorbell rang. Helen opened the door to see Edgar. For a moment, his gall shocked her but she quickly remembered he had no sense of right or wrong. He walked past her into the living room and eyed the cocktail glasses. "Isn't this cozy. Now I know why you were eager to keep me in jail."

Dan ignored Edgar's remark.

Helen compared the two men. Dan's face expressed a smirk. He had changed from his dark jacket to a cashmere sweater, blue like his eyes, while Edgar was dressed as usual in a dark suit, stiffly starched shirt and a tie. His face was flushed into splotches of red.

"What are you doing here, Edgar?" Helen asked.

He glared at her. "I came to take our daughter home."

Helen wished she could grab him and throw him out the door. "Not until August." With him being a suspect, she would find some way to prevent him from having Amy at any time.

Helen heard Guppy scratching the bedroom door and she opened it. Amy was asleep, but Guppy sprang out of the room. When the dog saw Edgar, he growled, bared his teeth and tugged at Edgar's pants. The scratching sound of fabric as it ripped. Edgar raised his foot to kick Guppy. Dan tackled Edgar and sat on him.

"Get off me," Edgar demanded.

Dan pulled a gun from his holster and coaxed Edgar to a chair. Helen's pulse beat like a metronome. She knew that in his job he had to be armed, but to actually see the gun in his hand made her shudder.

Dan said, "You realize the dog incriminated you."

"That damn pooch. I want a lawyer."

"As soon as you are booked."

Helen heard the bedroom doorknob twirl. She picked up Guppy and ran to meet Amy, blocking her view of the living area. Quickly, Helen tucked Amy and the dog into bed and closed the door behind her.

Dan's gun, which had shocked her at first, gave her courage to approach Edgar. "You were in from the beginning of the kidnap. How could you?"

"All I did was get rid of the mutt for them. I really wanted what was best for Amy," Edgar said. "I didn't mean to upset her."

Helen believed him because she realized that he was incapable of understanding the cost of his behavior. Knowing his weakness didn't alleviate her disgust with him. "Getting rid of the dog was a strange part to play. Was Roxanne better in bed than your secretary?"

A siren blared and stopped, followed by a pounding on the door. Helen rushed to open the door, fearing another knock would wake Amy.

Two policemen greeted her. Dan stood up and stretched. "Cuff him."

The older officer pulled out his handcuffs. "You had to call in the big guys, huh?"

The men became shadows, spinning in front of Helen. Poor Amy. Her father would be in jail, a criminal. Through the haze, she saw Dan walk out with the officers. She wanted to scream at the sight of Edgar in handcuffs. He had committed a crime and endangered his daughter. They were safer with him behind bars. The memory of possibilities that had deteriorated over the years into this present mess saddened Helen.

Before closing the door, she noticed a patch of dark blue sky punctuated with stars like rhinestone buttons on a gown. Edgar's criminal mind had finally caught up with him. Tomorrow would begin a new life for Amy and Helen.

When Dan returned, he handed Helen her partially finished drink and held his glass in a toast to her. "They want you to work in the security department."

Had she heard him right? "Stop kidding me. I am going back to work on the ship as soon as Amy has time to settle down and I figure out a sitter for her."

"It seems shipyard security was more impressed with your amateur investigating than I was. I agree with them. You are overqualified and overeducated to work on the ships"

"What would I be doing?

"Investigating." Dan laughed. "Pretty much what you did for Amy."

"But I made mistakes. You have a specialty and you trained for it."

"Your recent experience plus the supervision you will get is going to prepare you for the job as well, if not better, than the training I had."

Helen remembered feeling emboldened when she had discovered criminal activity. She would be good at this. "You're right. When are the authorities going to offer me the job?"

Dan kissed her. Helen kissed back. Her body tingled from her heart down to her toes. They sat on the small sofa, their bodies tangled and, for that moment, Helen dared to think that she was happier than she had been in years. Amy was safe in bed and Dan was exciting.

"You will be working for me. I have just hired you."

Helen stood up. "Let me tell you, I am not ready for a relationship, so don't expect me to be grateful to you."

Dan pulled her down next to him. He kissed her again and said, "I will be grateful to work with you."

Helen felt as though she were floating.

"How about a real date tomorrow night?" Dan said.

"I'd like that." Helen paused. "I'd really like that, but let's wait for a week or so, depending on how Amy adjusts. Then I am going to see if Amy will spend the night with my parents. It's time for them to be involved in our life. I can handle that now."

Acknowledgments

Many people had an impact on this book and I am deeply grateful to them.

Malena Watrous, an impeccable editor, for her editing and for cheering me on. Amy Rennert for her continued faith in me and for sharing her wisdom. Heartfelt thanks to Dorothy Smith for designing a magnificent cover and typesetting.

To the tearoom writers, a superb critique group: Karen Bjorneby, Mera Granberg, Mary Hower, Kat Meltzer, Rikke Jorgenson, Mary Moore, and Janis Cooke Newman. And earlier to Adair Lara.

To Nancy Langendorf for critiquing and super story advice and my other readers Angie and Bob Irvine, Peggy Myers, Bernice Ellison, and Lynne and Gil De Vincenzi.

And much appreciation to Kathy and John Abbot for technical advice and encouragement.

To the librarians at the Oregon Historical Society. No question was beyond their ability to find an answer. And the same gratitude to the librarians at Stanford and Palo Alto Libraries. And many thanks to George Fong, FBI unit chief, for his generosity of information.

L❶BRARY
PALO ALTO CITY

www.cityofpaloalto.org/library

Made in the USA
Charleston, SC
20 March 2010